THE MILL COTTAGE

THE MILL COTTAGE

Barbara Whitnell

This title first published in Great Britain 1998 by
SEVERN HOUSE PUBLISHERS LTD of
9–15 High Street, Sutton, Surrey SM1 1DF,
complete with new text by the author.
Originally published in 1982 in Great Britain by
Robert Hale Ltd under the name of *Ann Hutton*
and title of *Search For Simon.*
This title first published in the U.S.A. 1998 by
SEVERN HOUSE PUBLISHERS INC of
595 Madison Avenue, New York, N.Y. 10022.

British Library Cataloguing in Publication Data

Whitnell, Barbara
     The mill cottage
     1.   Romantic suspense novels
     I.   Title
     823.9'14 [F]

    ISBN 0-7278-2207-1

Printed and bound in Great Britain by
MPG Books Ltd, Bodmin, Cornwall.

ONE

As Lynn and I walked down the front steps towards the car I noticed that the daffodils under the trees at the far end of the lawn were beginning to show gleams of yellow. I had always loved the sight of them in the spring sunshine and the thought that they would soon be flowering in their full glory cheered me more than anything had done for some time.

"Look," I said to Lynn. "See the daffodils?"

She smiled.

"Marvellous, isn't it? Good old Mother Nature goes on producing the goods even after a disastrous year like this one. One might feel that the world is coming to an end, but it never does."

I looked at her, quickly and covertly. Her honey-blonde hair was caught up in a knot on the back of her head and she looked youthful and full of hope — an appearance that seemed at variance with the note of sadness in her voice.

"Things can only get better," I said. "At least you're doing a job you enjoy. The Chinese say that three years' bad luck is invariably followed by seven years' good luck, so perhaps we're both about to start collecting."

She lifted an eyebrow as if dubious of such an occurrence.

"Sarah, do you remember that ghastly dinner party you came to, before Max and I broke up," she said, with apparent inconsequence. "We talked about luck then."

5

"So we did."

Now that she mentioned it, I remembered the occasion well. It marked the date when I had given up all pretence of trying to like Maxwell Thurston, the man with whom my sister had so inexplicably fallen in love.

He was a sleek, handsome man with a ready smile, but in spite of his obvious charms I had never felt comfortable with him, though I struggled to give every appearance of liking him for my sister's sake. My parents, who were both alive at the time of Lynn's marriage, had felt the same.

"He's not right for her, Sarah," my father had said to me once in a burst of candour shortly before the wedding. "I'm not happy about it. There's a hard, ruthless streak in him."

Max and Lynn had lived in the Essex countryside not too far from our childhood home, in a lovely old Georgian house which she had restored with taste and care, plus a great deal of money. That, at least, was a commodity Max had never stinted. Love, attention, consideration – all these had been in incredibly short supply from the first, but never money. He was Sales Director in a family business which supplied parts to motor manufacturers and was constantly dashing over to Cologne or Paris or Turin and equally constantly entertaining Continental associates at home.

That night, I remembered, he had announced with his usual self-satisfaction that there was no such thing as bad luck.

"People make their own," he said. "I shouldn't be drinking brandy like this in a house like this if I hadn't worked for it."

"You've worked, that's true," Lynn agreed. "But you've had the breaks as well."

6

"Such as a wife like you, my darling."

Max had raised his glass to her, but his eyes were cold and unsmiling. Lynn returned his look stonily and I had the feeling that some unheard, quite different conversation was going on between them.

"Actually," Max continued, "it was my late father-in-law I had in mind." I felt my nerve-ends tighten. At that time my father had been dead for less than a year and I still ached with the loss of him and knew that Lynn felt the same. I was already aware of Max's low opinion of his business acumen and was in no mood to listen to more derogatory remarks about him.

"My father was very much loved," Lynn said tightly.

"Oh, certainly. No one's disputing that. But when it came to business, he was a babe in arms." He turned in explanation to the other members of the party. "My father-in-law had a thriving little business, but he allowed himself to be swindled —"

"He trusted people!"

"He trusted to luck. He didn't check up on his accountant and he paid the price. And what did everyone say? 'Bad luck, old boy!' Absolute nonsense! It was bad management, that's all."

"There were extenuating circumstances," I said, keeping a tight rein on my anger. "The accountant had been known to my father for years. They were close friends. The man behaved despicably, of course, but in some ways it *was* bad luck. He embezzled the money because of his son's illness. It was quite out of character for him to be dishonest."

My memory of that night did not extend to the way the conversation ended. Probably some other guest had been as struck as I had been by the bad taste of Max's remarks and had tactfully introduced

7

another topic. I had been left with the sure knowledge that Max Thurston was among my least favourite people.

"It was a very grand party," I said now to Lynn as I walked towards the car. "I remember that much."

"Pierre Cloutier was over from Paris. Remember him? A dark, clever-looking little man with a hooked nose. Max wanted to make a special impression on him. That's why we asked you. You were supposed to charm him."

"I was?" Frowning I searched my memory for Pierre Cloutier and found nothing. "I can't have done it very well."

"He preferred blondes, apparently. The wretched man propositioned me a dozen times that weekend."

"Max can't have been too pleased."

"Oh, all was permissible in the sacred name of business. Max was annoyed with me for not succumbing to his charm. He took it as one further example of my lack of co-operation in the pursuit of wealth. Sarah, there's something we haven't talked about this weekend and now I've left it too late."

She bent down and peered in through the car window as I belted myself into my seat.

"What's that?"

"This house. I don't want to stay here. There are just too many memories — and, anyway, it's far too big for me."

I sat and looked through the windscreen at the house in front of me. It was nothing special — just a red brick box with bay windows and a garden far too large for Lynn to manage on her own. It made no sense to hang on to it, yet it had been our home for most of our lives and now that so much had changed it seemed to be the one constant factor in an otherwise unstable world.

"You're right, of course," I said. "Look around for something more suitable."

I think I sounded brisk enough, but I couldn't help feeling a pang. Even the house, I thought as I drove away. Everything gone. No such thing as bad luck! Was Max right — or was there some terrible curse on my family that brought one disaster after another?

Don't be an idiot, I scolded myself as I went through the lanes towards the main road. It was wrong to think that way. We'd been through an unspeakably bad time, but so had plenty of other people, one way or another. Things were improving, at least where Lynn was concerned. Max was out of her life. She liked her new job. Her self-esteem was gradually recovering after being reduced to tatters by three years of marriage.

Of course she wanted to leave the house. It must be full of ghosts. Our mother had suffered a long and debilitating illness before she died there. Father, in his turn, had simply fallen asleep in his chair and had not woken up again, just as though he had lost all interest and purpose in life without either his wife or his business to sustain him.

And then there was Simon.

Why hadn't we talked of Simon? Not once, that whole weekend, had Lynn or I mentioned him — yet somehow it felt to me that we had never stopped talking of him. He was there, just around the corner of the landing or behind the closed door of his bedroom, or hidden from sight in the kitchen garden.

My throat closed up and my eyes began to sting. That's why neither of us spoke his name, I thought. We simply couldn't bear to. It was still too recent, too painful, even after six months — still quite unbelievable that he had really gone and that the house

9

would never echo his voice again.

He had been younger than either of us. The news that he had been killed in a tragic accident in France had shattered us completely.

He had sailed away so lightheartedly. If you're talking of luck, I thought, consider Simon — we'd always thought him the lucky one. He'd seemed to skate through life so effortlessly. Who could have imagined that an exploding gas cylinder would be the means of bringing all that vitality to an end? One enormous, annihilating bang — that's all it had taken to bring about the end of Simon, the yacht, and his two companions. The devastation had been total.

I forced my mind back to the daffodils. Time heals all things, I told myself. Spring was coming.

I was able to think about Simon quite calmly as I drove back to London. He had always been a rebel from his earliest days — always in trouble, always asking 'why?' He drove my parents to distraction but always seemed to get away with murder because he could always make them laugh even when they were angry.

He had been five years younger than Lynn, only eighteen months younger than I, which meant that he and I had been thrown together. I was always Maid Marion to his Robin Hood, Indian Maid to his Lone Ranger. I allowed myself to be tied up, half drowned, sworn at and led astray in more ways than my parents would have dreamed possible. Sometimes he made me cry, but more often he reduced me to helpless giggles — usually in church or some other inconvenient place, which would earn me a stern frown from my pious mother. It always seemed unfair to me that it was I and not Simon who earned the rebuke.

We could communicate with a silent look across a room. We laughed at the same off-beat things and as we grew up we shared a love of books and art and music. I adored him most of the time, thought him a pest some of the time and stood up for him all the time, for he was often in trouble.

He was the despair of my father as he grew up. My mother was, perhaps, less critical but this was mainly because she was already an invalid, which seemed to detach her from the day-to-day hurly-burly of life.

She did her best to make peace between her men-folk, but Simon's refusal to conform to Dad's ideas led to constant battles. Naturally, being the brightest of the lot of us, Simon was expected to pass exams and go to university, but this he consistently refused to do. His ambition was to write, but meantime he drove a lorry or worked as a hospital porter or dug holes in roads, which to my father's conservative mind were simply not done by young men of good education.

I think he would have made it as a writer. He had written scripts of plays for the three of us to perform and was a marvellous storyteller. To think of his talent being thrown away was an additional sadness.

It had been last June when he told me he was going sailing. I'd found him on the doorstep of my flat one Friday night when I got back from the department store where I worked in the Fine Art department. It had been a hot, airless evening and he had been wearing jeans and a T-shirt with 'Disney World' written on it. I greeted him with delight before remarking on his attire.

"When were you ever in Disney World?" I asked

him. He'd looked down at his chest vaguely as if reading the legend for the first time.

"I think it belongs to Mac," he said, referring to a Scottish mate who had been working on a building-site with him. "Well, he's had it now. I've left the site, Sarah, and I'm off to foreign parts. How about that?"

"How foreign?"

"Like French. Well, France to start with, I gather, then maybe on to Italy. I've come to say goodbye."

"You'd better come in and have a drink," I said. "You look hot."

"Well, I can't stop long, but I could certainly do an awful lot of damage to a can of beer, if you happen to have one handy. I finished work at lunchtime and dashed up to get some last-minute things — what a sweat! There's no place worse than London when it's as hot as this."

He followed me inside the flat and collapsed into an armchair, which creaked ominously.

"Do treat that with respect," I begged. "It's rather elderly. You can't expect much for two pounds fifty. Did you drive up?"

"Yes — mm, that beer's good. I'm parked just round the corner by the Chinese takeaway. I must say this area isn't what one would term salubrious, is it?"

"I'd rather live here on my own than somewhere upmarket with a gaggle of girls."

"Pity you can't find a wealthy husband, like Lynn."

We had been conversing at some distance, he in the tiny living-room, me in the slit-like kitchen, but at this I put my head round the door.

"Look what it did for her! A disaster from the start, if ever I saw one. Lynn didn't marry Max for his money, though. She was genuinely in love with

12

him at the time."

Simon looked pensive as he swigged his beer.

"Amazing, isn't it? I always thought him the most awful stuffed shirt, and an unpleasant stuffed shirt at that. Do you think she will really divorce him?"

"Yes, I think so. I hope so. He's so — destructive of her. Heaven knows, I've tried to like him, as befits a good sister-in-law, but it was an unequal struggle. To me, he's pure poison. But never mind Max — tell me about this trip of yours."

"I met the guys I'm going with through Max, actually. He's a strange bloke, Sal. He didn't want me to go with them. It was almost as if he resented them being friendly."

"I didn't know you saw him these days. Where did you meet them?"

"Last night at the Sailing Club. Max phoned to say would I care to crew for him —"

"Ha! You don't like the man, but you'll accept a sail from him."

"As befits a good brother-in-law. It was marvellous on the Blackwater last night. I was fantasising about how great it would be just to sail away into the sunset, never to set foot on that blasted building-site again, when suddenly the chance to do just that literally fell into my lap. There were a couple of Max's mates in the bar. We had a few beers together and they told me they were about to leave for a holiday in the Med. A third chap was supposed to be going too, but he'd had a car crash and broken his leg that very afternoon, so they offered me the chance to go with them."

"How do you know you'll get on with them?" I asked. "It's close quarters on a boat."

"They were all right. I get on with most people."

"Even so, it sounds risky."

He pulled a face at me.

13

"Unlike you, I don't shun my fellow men."

"Nor do I!" My voice soared indignantly. "I've got loads of friends. Just because I enjoy my privacy, I'm not exactly a hermit. I can't think of anything worse than being closeted in a small space with people I don't know."

"They're all right," he said again. "It was odd, though, the way Max tried to talk me out of it."

"Which, I have no doubt, made you all the more determined to go! Maybe he knows something about them that you don't."

"Well, I tackled him after we'd gone but he refused to say anything other than that they weren't my type, which cut no ice with me, since I don't think he has any idea what 'my type' is."

He had left soon after that, and I had not seen him again.

He had posted a card to me from Marseilles.

"Hate to admit it but you were right and I was wrong," he had written. "One boat not big enough for the three of us. Am transhipping and proceeding to Cannes and points east with a pair of highly congenial North Sea divers. Keep the wheels of commerce turning. The waters of the Med are azure, as is the sky. PS. What's work? I vaguely remember it, as from a previous existence."

It was the last communication we had from him.

I was almost glad when a thin drizzle began to fall. It meant that I had to concentrate exclusively on driving, for the conditions were difficult and the build-up of traffic enormous as I approached the City. There was no opportunity to dwell on the past. Instead, I kept my mind firmly in the present as I drove across London and finally turned into the rear of the news-agent's shop in Putney, above which was my flat.

14

The fact that I had it to myself was, perhaps, its only advantage, but it was one that meant a lot to me. I had taken a great pride in decorating it and had searched junk shops in order to furnish it. I always liked getting back to it after being away.

Usually my weekends at home lasted until Sunday evening, but on that occasion I had returned earlier than usual because there were a number of chores I wanted to do before Monday morning. There was some ironing, some letters to write. But first I assembled a small snack in my tiny kitchen and took a tray through to the living-room, where I switched on the television.

The early news bulletin had already started. I'd meant to watch it from the beginning, but as I listened to the catalogue of gloom and doom I began to be rather sorry I had switched it on at all. One day, I told myself, I'm going to find me a desert island, miles away from civilisation, where there are no strikes, no demonstrations, no politicians. And, just possibly, I added somewhat wryly, not a lot of fun either. Still, it would be nice if just once in a way there could be some good news to report.

As if in answer to my unspoken plea, the news-caster's expression seemed to lighten.

"And finally, a happy ending to the hunt for the small boy that has been going on throughout the whole of the south-west this weekend," he said. "Volunteer helpers turned out in their hundreds to help the police search for young Danny Ware, who disappeared from his home in Plymouth on Tuesday. It was feared that Danny had been abducted, but instead he was found late last night alive and well, sheltering in a fish warehouse in Poldrissick in Cornwall. It appears that he enjoyed his holiday there so much that he couldn't wait until next summer to go back. . ."

I missed the rest of the item.

15

Poldrissick, I was thinking. Poldrissick. I knew that I was smiling, though in a way I felt more like crying, for we had been so happy there, the whole family, a million years ago.

Memories flooded back to me. Simon had been twelve, learning to sail. Lynn had conceived a romantic passion for a fisherman, whilst I had been spotty and gangling and unsure in which world I belonged. I'd been happiest running around with Simon, I remembered, yet I'd insisted on dressing up and going to a dance with Lynn, much to her annoyance. No one had asked me to dance and I'd hated every agonising moment of it.

There was Poldrissick on the screen. Oh, how I'd loved it! All of it — even the screeching of the seagulls that woke me each morning. I remembered the white caps on blue, whippy waves, and the cottages clustered round the harbour, rising one on top of the other. There they were, just the same as ever, and the fishing-boats, riding at anchor.

The parents, tearful with joy, were being interviewed on the quayside, and were expressing their thanks to all the people who had helped in the search, but I wasn't listening properly. I was far too busy looking at the background scenery.

So young and carefree and unaware, I thought. I wished so much that I could go back. Back to Poldrissick? Well, yes, but that wasn't entirely what I meant. I sighed, knowing that never would I be able to return to quite that state of innocent bliss.

And then I saw him.

My heart gave a great leap and I gasped with shock. On the edge of the picture a young man had appeared dressed in a polo-necked sweater, blue jeans and a duffle coat. He had walked towards the reporter from a point somewhere behind him, his gaze intent on a paper in his hand. He checked at the sudden sight of the knot of people, flicked a startled gaze towards the camera, then hastily walked on.

It had taken only the barest fraction of a second. His hair was longer than I remembered, his face perhaps a little thinner, but even so there was no doubt in my mind. It was Simon — my brother Simon, reported dead after an explosion in quite another harbour, hundreds of miles away. But not dead — not dead at all.

With my heart pounding and my fingers trembling so much that I could hardly dial the numbers, I reached for the telephone to call Lynn.

TWO

Naturally, she didn't believe me.

"They say everyone has a double," she said.

"Lynn, it wasn't just the way he looked. There was something quite unmistakable about the way he walked and moved his head."

"He was on your mind, wasn't he? I'll bet anything you were thinking of him on the way home."

"I was," I agreed, sobering slightly. Was it possible that I had been mistaken? It was such a quick glimpse and now that it was over my certainty seemed to be evaporating with every second that passed. How could I be so sure it was Simon when the whole incident had been over in a second? Then I remembered the stiff-legged, bouncy stride that was typical of him when he was in a hurry. "Even so —" I went on.

"Sarah, don't raise your hopes, for heaven's sake. It's impossible, you must see that. What would he be doing in Poldrissick, of all places? If he were alive and safe anywhere in the world, surely he would let us know?"

That aspect of the case was, of course, unanswerable. If the young man I had seen *was* Simon, why had he not rushed to a telephone at the first possible moment after the accident to contact his family? Why had he allowed us to suffer for so many months? As Lynn said, it was impossible. And yet —

"Loss of memory?" I hazarded feebly.

There was silence between us. Then I sighed, reluctant to give up the wonderful idea that Simon was alive but acknowledging after all that I must have been mistaken.

"You're right," I said. "It's all quite crazy. Still, look at the late bulletin, won't you? Just in case."

"Of course. I don't hold out any hope, though."

The news on a Sunday night was at ten minutes past ten. Once again I sat through the catalogue of disasters that constituted the bulletin. I prayed that the item would not have been dropped and was rewarded by a rerun of the scene at Poldrissick. There was the harbour and the boats at anchor. A wind was blowing. The mother of the little boy was young and dark with a West Country accent and long hair that kept whipping across her face. Eagerly I leaned forward, not daring to breathe, waiting for the moment when the young man came into view.

He was there, and he was gone. Still I sat, staring unseeingly at the screen, not hearing the closing sentences of the bulletin, seeing only the familiar thrust of the shoulders and the self-confident turn of his head. The telephone rang as I knew it would.

"I saw him," Lynn said breathlessly.

"It was Simon, wasn't it? I wasn't mistaken."

"It's impossible!"

"But you agree with me?"

"I don't know what to think. But, yes — I do agree that if it wasn't Simon it was someone uncannily like him. He was even wearing the sweater I gave him for Christmas a couple of years ago."

"But why, Lynn? Why hasn't he contacted us? Should we phone the police or someone in Poldrissick and tell them, just in case he *has* lost his memory?"

"No," Lynn said quickly. I frowned.

"What, then?"

"I don't know. Look, Sarah, let's sleep on it, and I'll ring you tomorrow. Perhaps between us we can think of what's best to do."

19

Sleep on it, she said. I only wished that I could, for I tossed and turned, doubts and theories chasing themselves in my mind, none of them making any sense at all. The sky was already growing lighter when at last I fell into a troubled sleep.

"We must tell the police," I said when Lynn phoned the following day. "They would be able to find out if someone answering to Simon's description had been in Poldrissick recently. It's only a tiny place."

"No," Lynn said.

"But, Lynn, there was the inquiry and all the investigation that went on at the time. The case was never closed satisfactorily. They ought to be told, quite apart from the fact that they might be able to help us."

"No." Her voice was even more decisive than before. I waited a second or two for her to elaborate on this monosyllable, but there was silence.

"What, then?" I asked, a trifle testily. "Short of going down there ourselves —"

"That would be far better."

"Well, perhaps. But I can't see you wanting to take time off now that you've just started a new job, and I can't get away . . .

My voice trailed away because even as I spoke, I was thinking that it wouldn't be so difficult to get away after all. I had leave owing to me that had to be taken before the beginning of May. No one else in the department was away just then, and it was a fairly quiet time of year.

"I don't know," I went on. "I suppose I could take a few days. But why not bring in the police, Lynn? I don't understand your objections."

"Simon might not welcome it."

I was shocked into silence and then I laughed.

"You mean he might be a fugitive from justice, or

20

something? Don't be an ass, Lynn! Simon isn't capable of doing anything wrong — well, not *that* wrong."

"He was always a law unto himself."

"Yes, but only in minor, unimportant ways. He'd never hurt anyone or be dishonest." I pulled up short as a thought struck me. "Surely you don't think that he was responsible for blowing up the yacht, do you? I mean, even by accident?"

"I don't know what I think except that supposedly he was blown up in Cannes harbour six months ago, and now it appears that he wasn't at all. Neither of us has any idea what he's been up to since he left England with those two men from the Sailing Club."

"We know that he left them."

"Yes."

Although Lynn was apparently agreeing with me, a question hung in the air. She sounded as if she was about to say more, but nothing came. I waited a bit, then suggested that she should come up to town so that we could tak about it face to face.

"I'll come after work tomorrow," she said.

I bought the makings of a meal and found that she was waiting for me when I returned home, just as Simon had been on that last evening the previous summer. The chops remained ungrilled, however, as we talked over the question from all angles. She was unswerving in her certainty that we should on no account bring the police into it. Simon, she said over and over again, might have good reason for dropping out.

"I wish I knew what you had in mind," I said.

"I haven't anything particular in mind. It's just that those two men Simon went sailing with were friends of Max's — and, believe me, Sarah, Max had some very funny friends."

21

"What sort of funny?"

"Well, you know — maybe not dishonest, exactly, but not honest either. People who would do anything for a tax-free profit. He was odd and inconsistent really, because he was very strong on appearances — having the right sort of house, joining the right clubs, wearing the right sort of clothes. All that sort of thing. Yet there was this strange kind of underside to his life, with people he never brought home. I remember a ghastly fat, greasy sort of a man who drove a Rolls the size of a house. We met him quite by chance in a pub and he knew Max well — but Max was as embarrassed as all-get-out to introduce him to me. He sat with us and talked non-stop for what seemed ages about the various fiddles he'd been smart enough to pull off. Max tried to pass it off afterwards by saying he hardly knew the man, but I could tell that wasn't true." She sighed heavily as if talking about those days had brought back to her the slow disillusion of her marriage.

"There were others as well," she went on after a moment. "I never dared enquire too deeply into the way he was running the business — the means he used to acquire orders. There was one occasion — the whole of one weekend — when there was a terrible panic. I knew Max was frightened to death. The phone never stopped ringing. I had no idea what it was all about and Max refused to talk about it, but I knew in my heart of hearts that he'd done something or other that he was terrified would come out in the open."

I stared at her in horror.

"Lynn, how awful for you! I didn't have any idea of that."

"How could you? But you see why I feel we ought to walk warily now. I just feel scared to death that Simon might have got himself caught up in some of

Max's dirty work."

"But he'd *left* those men. I never did know their names."

Lynn shrugged helplessly.

"I know. I know it doesn't really make sense. I suppose it's simply that having lived with Max I seem to have lost my simple, childlike trust in human nature. I'd much rather try to find Simon ourselves before blowing the whistle on him."

I sighed.

"Which means me, I suppose, since you can't get away. I made a few inquiries today and it seems that I can take leave any time during the next couple of weeks, just so long as I'm back by the end of the month when the boss flies off to the sun. I wish you could come, Lynn."

"So do I – but truly, I can't even bring myself to ask. Heavens above, I haven't worked a full month yet and we're terribly busy."

I accepted the inevitable. For good or ill, it seemed that this was something I should have to do on my own, though I felt distinctly nervous about my abilities as a sleuth. How on earth did one start looking for someone, if one ruled out going to the police? I should have to furnish myself with a photograph of Simon, that much was obvious. At least Poldrissick was only a small village, which must surely make my task easier.

I finally cooked the meal and, shortly afterwards Lynn left. I sat for a while thinking of practicalities – whether I should book a room or leave it to chance; if it would be a good idea to get the car serviced before embarking on such a long journey. Then, suddenly, the enormity of it hit me afresh and I gasped, hunched up in my chair, suffering all over again the shock of seeing Simon on the television

23

screen.

Why, why, why? I asked myself, over and over again. For what possible reason could he want to make a new life for himself – a life in which he wanted no contact with his family or previous friends?

It hurt – it hurt me very much, for we had been so close. How could he do it? It wasn't like him. He must have known what reports of his death would do to Lynn and me, coming on top of the loss of both our parents. How could he possibly have let us mourn him the way we had done?

Loss of memory? Was that really a possibility? One would like to think so. It happened, of course. People received bangs on the head and woke up remembering nothing of their past. But in view of the investigations that had gone on after the explosion, it seemed unlikely. Someone, somewhere, would have come to his aid, always supposing that by some miracle he had been thrown clear of the yacht and had awoken suffering from amnesia. Someone would have taken him to a hospital or the police or the British Embassy.

Wearily I went to my bed, my previous sleepless night finally catching up on me, and this time I slept soundly and peacefully. It was only when I awoke in the morning that the knot of nervousness formed in my stomach again, and somewhat to my surprise I realised that having always thought of myself as self-sufficient and highly independent, I longed more than anything for someone to share this burden with me.

Everything, I thought drearily, depends on me. It was a thought I found anything but cheering.

THREE

I felt better once I had started on my journey a couple of days later. I always enjoyed driving and this was a perfect day on which to do it, for the sun was shining and the little cotton-wool clouds looked benign and decorative in the eggshell blue sky. I hoped my mother knew how much enjoyment I extracted from the little hatchback car I had bought with the legacy she left me. Having my own wheels spelled freedom and independence for me and although I couldn't really afford to run it, I would have worn sackcloth for a year to keep it on the road.

I avoided the motorway and drove across Salisbury Plain, exulting in the space and the greenness all about me. I loved the glimpses of towns and villages, the spring flowers in the gardens that I passed, the children playing a singing game in the yard of a school. I even waited in perfect contentment as a herd of cows milled around me on their way from one field to another. I was quite happy, just to be in the countryside, away from the noise and grime of London.

Odd doubts assailed me, of course. There were moments when I felt quite certain I was on a fool's errand, that both Lynn and I must have been misled by a remarkable likeness, but deliberately I kept my mind on the road and the scenery. I had armed myself with a photograph of Simon in which he was dressed in jeans and sweater and looked very similar to the way he had appeared on the screen. Until I reached Poldrissick there was nothing more I could do.

25

The scenery was beautiful all the way, but particularly so, I thought, from Exeter to Plymouth where green wooded hills and valleys smiled in the spring sunlight. I stopped for petrol just short of Plymouth and felt a warm flow of delight at the sound of the garage attendant's voice. It underlined for me quite unmistakably the distance I had travelled from London.

"'Tis an 'andsome day, m'dear," the man said, and I agreed that indeed it was.

I had no idea what my stay in Cornwall would hold for me but as I crossed the Tamar bridge I knew that I had been right to come and found it hard to understand why, in all the twelve years that had elapsed since our holiday there, I had not visited it again. There had been other places to see, of course. I had gone on school trips and on exchange visits with foreign students. We had camped in France and sailed in Greece, but we had never taken our holiday in Cornwall again.

With the sun shooting sparks from the dancing waves I had to remind myself that it was not always like this. It rained a lot in the south-west and could be grey and dismal, but on that day I thought I had seen nothing lovelier in Europe than the sight of the green hills sloping down to the river where vessels of all sizes sheltered in its waters, from small dinghies to a mighty aircraft carrier.

And then at last I was in Cornwall and suddenly the doubts I had been holding back all day flooded in like the tide. I must be mad, I thought. Although identification of the bodies had been impossible, there had never been the slightest doubt that Simon had perished in the explosion. The hope that had buoyed me up suddenly seemed vain and empty and all I could feel now was a premonition of the cold disappointment that I felt certain was in store for me.

Soberly I completed the last lap of my journey, which seemed endless. As if the elements were in tune with my mood, the sun disappeared. I missed my way some miles beyond Truro, which added considerably to my journey. By the time I managed to find the road to Poldrissick — a village which the makers of signposts seemed to have overlooked altogether — I was tired and dispirited, but my heart lifted as I drove down the narrow hill into the village, for it seemed little changed since our previous visit. I had dreaded to find it full of ice-cream parlours and gift shops. It was, of course, too early in the season for many tourists to have found their way to it and it hardly seemed to have woken from its winter sleep. Perhaps in a month or two all would be different. For now, it looked much as I remembered it — except for a large sign telling drivers to leave their cars outside the harbour area, as the streets were narrow and twisted.

Dutifully, I obeyed the instruction, left my case locked inside the boot and walked the few remaining yards to the village square. Gulls were screaming overhead, just as I remembered, and there, at the corner of the square, was the group of rubber-booted fishermen, laughing and gossiping just as they always had done. Surely not the same men, I thought. Well, perhaps not, but they looked no different.

The Anchor Inn stood in the square and I decided to try for a bed there. It struck me that it might be a good centre for village gossip and it also seemed likely that should Simon be in the area he might well make his way there sooner or later.

But before I went into the inn I walked down a narrow alley which led from the square to the harbour. It smelled of fish and seaweed. The two piers, one short, one long, enclosed the small collection of boats like sheltering arms, and on the retaining wall there were nets drying, and lobster-pots. Close to the village, houses climbed the cliff, huddled together as if for warmth. I shivered. I could do with a little of that myself, I thought.

To the right of the harbour the cliffs fell into a narrow, spiny finger that jutted into the sea, and to the left — the side from which Simon had made his appearance — they degenerated into a jumble of rocks. My spirits rose a little. It was indeed a very small village. Even if Simon had merely been staying here for a night or two, it seemed likely that someone would remember him.

I retraced my steps to the inn, where I found a plump and friendly landlady who was only too pleased to show me the inn's one room. It was small and cold with a single-bar electric fire. One wall was painted in a distressing shade of salmon pink while the other three were covered in purple roses. A large double bed with a slippery gold eiderdown almost filled the room. I could tell at a glance that this would undoubtedly slide to the floor at the first opportunity, but the room, if hideous, was spotlessly clean and I had no hesitation in saying that I would take it — 'for several nights', I said vaguely.

"If that's all right," I added hastily. "I'm not quite certain how long I want to stay."

The landlady, Mrs Watkin by name, was agreeable.

"Tha'ss all right, my love," she said, beaming. "Easter being late this year, we'm not properly open till the end of the month. 'Tis different story then. We've got bookings all through till September-time, but you'm more than welcome to stay just now." There was a questioning look in her eye as she surveyed me. "On your own, are you?"

"Yes."

My reply seemed abrupt after her almost effusive speech and to make up for it I delved into my bag for Simon's photograph.

"I'm looking for my brother, actually," I said. "He's thought to be staying somewhere in Poldrissick. Maybe you've seen him."

She took the picture from me and studied it with attention, her lips pursed. She had a comfortable, cottage-loaf figure and a kindly face, and she seemed genuinely sorry not to be able to help me.

"No, my love," she said, handing the photograph back to me. "Can't say as how I've seen un. But you ask my husband when you go downstairs to the bar — he knows everyone, Jack does. Run away from home, has he?"

I hesitated, then nodded. It was pointless even beginning to tell the whole story.

"No consideration, young people today," she said. "My sister's boy was the same. Never a word once he got to London. Yes, you ask Jack. He'll know where to find un, if anyone does. Could you fancy a nice fried mackerel?"

I could, and said as much.

"There's only the kitchen to eat in, mind, but you'm welcome to what we've got."

I assured her that I would, above all things, like to eat in the kitchen. Whatever else, I thought, it would surely be warm. I went back to the car-park to get my case and returned to the Anchor to wash and tidy up a little, wasting as short a time as possible in the Arctic atmosphere of my room before descending to the kitchen, which was every bit as cosy as I had hoped. The mackerel was delicious and so was the apple pie and clotted cream that followed. Mrs Watkin, washing glasses at the sink, accompanied my meal with a non-stop monologue on the subject of the village and its amenities, the habits of summer visitors, and the compliments paid to her by her 'regulars', who returned year after year. I was not called upon to do more than nod and smile at intervals.

Eventually, the meal over, I made my way to the bar. A large, florid man was serving and he, I assumed, was Jack Watkin, licensed to sell beers, wines and spirits. He amiably poured me a gin-and-tonic, but as he was already engaged in a spirited (and to me largely unintelligble) conversation with a weatherbeaten fisherman, I did not speak to him about Simon just then but contented myself with looking about me.

The sea motif was everywhere in evidence. There was a wealth of glass floats and anchors and ships' wheels. Lanterns hung from the beams above the bar — red on the port side, green on the starboard. The small fragments of wallpaper which were all that was visible between these nautical decorations bore a pattern of seahorses.

All the customers at the bar looked like men of the sea, wind-tanned and tough as weathered rock. They conversed in loud voices which sounded as if they were more used to combating the noise of a high wind rather than exchanging social chit-chat. They were of different ages and sizes, but all looked at me with some curiosity, nodding a cautious greeting over the rims of their glasses.

Jack Watkin was full of jokes and laughter and camaraderie and obviously enjoyed an amicable relationship with his customers. He did indeed appear the sort of man who knew everybody. I bided my time, waiting for the opportunity to speak to him, feeling conspicuous by staying at the bar, which was so obviously a male preserve. There were two other women present in the room with their attendant

30

menfolk, but they were sitting at some remove from the bar.

"Excuse me," I said at last, finding him near to me and at last unengaged. "Your wife said she thought you might be able to help me."

"Oh? Always ready to oblige a pretty young lady, that's right, eh, Tom?" He grinned at a grizzled old man who was close beside me but as he turned again to look at me I thought that his eyes looked wary, as if the smiles and the bonhomie were only surface deep.

Tom wheezed appreciatively and made some reply in an accent so broad that I did not immediately understand him. When light dawned, I thought it prudent to continue to feign ignorance. Tom's humour was, to say the least, of the earthy variety. Again I produced Simon's photograph.

"This is my brother," I said. "He's been missing for some time, but we heard he was seen here. I wondered if you happened to know where I could find him."

The landlord gave the snapshot what I considered an unnecessarily cursory glance.

"Never seen un," he said briefly, handing it back to me.

"'Ere, give us a squint at un," said old Tom, holding out his hand. "Your brother, eh? I dunno, I may 'ave seen un. Look's familiar, some'ow. Bill, ever clapped eyes on this chap?"

The photograph was passed from hand to hand. One thought it looked the spitting image of his sister Mabel's boy, the one that went to Australia, while another said it put him in mind of an announcer chap on the telly. A younger man with dark curly hair looked at it, frowning with concentration, and said that he was certain he'd seen Simon somewhere, but

31

he was damned if he could remember where.

"Give us another look," Tom said. "I'll do it with me specs on this time. Cor, some difference that makes, my bird. I know now where I seen un to — 'twas in Beswarick's shop, the morning all them TV people and police and whatnot was down on the quay."

"Last Sunday?"

"Tha'ss right. Mrs Beswarick opens for an hour or two of a Sunday morning and I'd gone in for me papers and baccy. Some funny we thought it was."

"Funny? Why?"

"Well, my lover, 'twas like this, see. This young chap comes in with 'is fancy accent asking for all manner of stuff — eggs, butter, cheese and all sorts. When the reckoning was made, damme if he was short of cash and couldn't pay! 'Ad to leave 'alf of it be'ind! 'Ad a good laugh, the rest of us did."

That definitely had to be Simon, I thought with rueful amusement. He never could add up.

"Do you know where he was staying?"

Tom shook his head.

"Never seen un before nor since," he said.

The saloon bar was filling up now and Jack Watkin was busy pulling a pint with his back towards me so that I could not see his face as he spoke.

"He's your brother, you say?" His voice sounded neutral and non-committal, but when he turned to put the foaming tankard on the bar he looked at me with an appraising expression.

He doesn't believe me, I thought in astonishment. But why not, in heaven's name? Does he think I'm a wife trying to track down a runaway husband or something? I put the photograph back in my bag and turned once again to Tom.

"If you should happen to see him again, please tell

32

him that his sister is anxious to get in touch with him, won't you?"

"Arr — I'll do that, my bird," Tom assured me.

I stood a round of drinks and feeling as though I had learnt as much as I was likely to, I said good-night and made for the door. Before I reached it I felt a touch on my shoulder and turned to see that the younger, curly-haired man who had looked longest at Simon's picture had detached himself from the group at the bar and had followed me.

"Couldn't we talk?" he asked me. "I might be able to help you."

"Could you?"

I looked at him for a moment, assessing whether he had something to tell me or if this was a simple pick-up. He was smiling at me, his teeth very white against his brown skin. Put a ring in his ear and he'd look like a pirate, I thought. Oh, well — so what if this was a pick-up? It could hardly lead to a fate worse than death merely to talk to him in a crowded saloon bar, and who knows, I might learn something. He led me to a table in the corner.

"That photograph," he said. "It bothers me. I feel sure I've seen the man somewhere, but I can't remember where."

"Have another look."

He did so, then placed the picture flat on the table in front of me like a playing-card. I looked at him questioningly, but he was still frowning, his eyes narrowed.

"Who is he?" he asked. "Why is he here?"

"If I knew that, half my problems would be over."

"What makes you think he's in Poldrissick?"

I explained that I had seen him on the television screen, still holding back on the fact that we had presumed him dead. He sat back in his chair, saying

33

nothing, puzzled eyes fixed on me, a thumbnail tapping against his teeth.

"Look, *do* you know anything? I asked him. "Can you throw any light on where he might be."

Slowly he shook his head.

"No," he said slowly. "No, I can't." There was something in his voice that made me raise my eyebrows questioningly. It was as if somehow light was beginning to dawn on him, in spite of his words.

"I don't know that I believe you," I said.

He grinned at me – a slow, teasing smile that in normal times I would have found hard to resist.

"That's your problem," he said. "I can't tell what I don't know."

I looked at him with exasperation, unable to tell from his manner if he was telling the truth.

"You're not Cornish, are you?" I asked him.

"'Ess, my lover." He adopted the accent common to most of the other men in the bar. "Born and brought up in Poldrissick. I joined the Navy and saw the world, though, just like they tell you."

"And now you're back?"

"Tha'ss right, my bird."

"All right – you've convinced me! Look, why don't you tell me what you know about my brother? I feel sure you've got some idea where he is –"

He laughed.

"I assure you I haven't, Miss – I don't think I heard your name."

"Kendall. Sarah Kendall."

"I'm Laurie Barron."

"What do you do with yourself now that you've left the Navy?"

"I fish and take tourists for trips around the bay in summer. A good life – if you don't mind not making a fortune. What about you?"

34

I told him about my job in the Fine Art department and heard my voice going on a little too long about some rare Chinese porcelain we had recently acquired, so stopped abruptly.

"You're pretty keen on your work," he commented.

"Well, of course."

"Are you a buyer?"

"I'm working my way up through the ranks."

"And your brother? Is he artful and crafty too?"

It was a joke, so dutifully I laughed. But was it? Laurie was smiling still, but there was that indefinable air of distrust about him. Abruptly I stood up, wearying of the feeling that he was playing cat-and-mouse with me.

"I'm awfully tired," I said. "Please excuse me. I think I'll have an early night."

I was telling no more than the truth. Weariness had suddenly engulfed me and even though I did not relish the thought of returning to that cold little room upstairs, I longed to close my eyes and forget my troubles until morning.

I said goodnight to Laurie Barron and made my getaway, and was overwhelmed with gratitude to find that Mrs Watkin had put a hot-water bottle in my bed. The world suddenly seemed a much friendlier place.

FOUR

I awoke in the same frame of mind to the sound of gulls — a noise which to me seemed to epitomise the atmosphere of Poldrissick like some form of signature tune. Illogically, considering I had received little help from anyone in the bar last night with the sole exception of Tom, I felt hopeful and encouraged. Simon had been seen shopping in Poldrissick less than a week ago, and shopping for basic provisions too, which seemed to imply that he was making more than a fleeting visit to the neighbourhood.

But why Poldrissick? Why should he have chosen this small enclosed little society in which to hide himself? In summer, when it overflowed with visitors, it seemed part of the great outside world. Now it was an outpost — a small community where not only did everyone know everyone else, but half of them were related to one another.

Could it possibly have been that, just like the small boy from Plymouth who had caused such a stir, he had gone back to the place where we had all been so happy?

I dismissed the idea as soon as it occurred to me. The house we had rented was outside the village, but not that far outside. Someone would certainly have known if a stranger had turned up there and by this time would have uncovered all there was to know about him. Poldrissick was like that. Nevertheless I decided that I would walk up to it — for old times' sake if for no other reason — as soon as I had finished breakfast.

An intermittent sun was shining in a temporary sort of way, but it was a pleasant enough morning as I set off up the hill out of the village. A row of terraced cottages fronted the street, many with window-boxes full of spring flowers adorning them. Two fishermen wearing canvas smocks over thick sweaters clumped down the hill towards the harbour and wished me good morning as they passed me. Everything seemed normal and friendly, as if the village held no secrets.

Yet it does, I thought. It does.

Every instinct I possessed told me that Laurie Barron was being less than frank with me, and Jack Watkin, too. Why had my story seemed so unbelievable to him? Surely it was feasible enough, that a young man had left home and that his family was searching for him?

The village ran out of houses and I was soon walking uphill between high banks, thick with primroses. A cow looked at me incuriously over a hedge.

At the top of the hill were crossroads where five lanes met, and for a moment I stood, irresolute. Now that it came to the point I found it hard to remember exactly which one to take. How incredible that seemed! For six whole weeks that house had been our home. For six whole weeks I had turned towards it, loving it, never wanting to leave it, yet now I couldn't remember if I should take the first or second lane on the right. Oh, well — twelve years was a long time, and things had changed. This road had surely been widened and houses had been built down there in the valley that had never been there before.

It was the second lane, I decided, and turned into it, recognising with delight that I had made the right choice, for here was the gate where one could lean and have a sight of the sea framed beautifully in a fold of the hills, and there was the barn where we had dicovered a family of kittens, and here the cottage which had sold eggs and honey. The sign still swung by the garden gate.

The house had been called Sea View for obvious reasons, and it still was. It stood back a little from the lane, but I could see that it was a great deal better cared for than when we had rented it. It had been freshly painted white and some sort of extension had been added on to the back.

The garden, a wilderness in our time, was tamed and full of flowers. Two small children were riding tricycles round and round a circular drive outside the front door and I could see that to the side of the house a young woman was pegging washing on the line. On impulse, not having meant to do anything of the kind, I opened the gate and walked in.

The children pedalled furiously towards me, calling out greetings in a friendly and uninhibited way, and at this their mother turned and saw me. She stopped what she was doing and came to meet me, a child's nightdress in her hands.

She was cheerful and welcoming and apparently politely interested in the fact that my family had once enjoyed a wonderful holiday under what was now her roof.

"It must have been quite a long time ago," she said. "We've lived here eight years and we bought it from an elderly couple who'd been here for some time before that."

"It was twelve years ago. We all loved it so much, but it was fairly dilapidated. You've improved it out of all recognition — especially the garden! It's beautiful."

"That's the most beautiful thing of all." She nodded towards the view of the sea, blue and placid in the

38

spring sunshine. "We moved here from London, and I still haven't got blasé about it, even after all these years."

"You're lucky to be able to live and work here."

"Yes, aren't we? My husband's the doctor. Look, would you like to see it inside? We've made a lot of changes there, too."

"Oh, I couldn't possibly bother you . . ."

She insisted that it was no bother at all and in fact seemed to take pleasure in showing me the improvements they had made, from the luxury kitchen with every modern appliance known to man to the new, wide windows in the sitting-room, the better to see the incomparable view.

I thanked her for all the trouble she had taken and said how interested I had been to see the house again.

"But I did have another reason for coming," I said. "I'm really looking for my brother. I don't suppose you happen to have seen him?"

I showed her the photograph, but she shook her head.

"I'm sorry," she said, sounding as if she meant it. "I can't help you at all. Did you really think he might have come back to this house? After twelve years?"

Yet again I returned the photograph to my wallet.

"I know it sounds silly. It was just a thought that occurred to me in the absence of any other ideas."

"What makes you think he's in Poldrissick?"

I explained about seeing Simon on television.

"What an extraordinary thing!"

"I know." Lady, I thought, you little know how extraordinary!

"A stranger at this time of the year sticks out like a sore thumb in Poldrissick. Perhaps he was only here for the day."

Buying eggs and butter and bread?

39

"Perhaps you're right," I agreed.

I thanked her again, but before leaving turned to look once more at the view.

"You really are lucky, you know," I said.

"Don't I know it! I hope you find your brother."

"Thank you. I hope the weather stays dry for your washing."

She laughed.

"I have the gravest doubts."

Outside the gate I stood irresolutely in the lane and wondered where now to direct my footsteps.

If only I could think myself into Simon's mind, I thought — where would I go? Where would he go?

The Mill Cottage!

Why on earth hadn't I thought of that before? My memory really was behaving in the most extraordinary way. It seemed as if everything that occurred to me had first to be suggested by something else. Things came back to me piecemeal, almost like reading a book I had read years before and largely forgotten.

Now, standing in the lane outside the house, it seemed the most natural thing in the world that Simon would have taken refuge in the Mill Cottage, yet until that point I had forgotten its existence.

Goodness knows, it was remote enough, and totally hidden from prying eyes. We had found it by accident. Simon was following a large-scale ordnance survey map — or rather, attempting to follow it — and had managed to get us hopelessly lost, although he kept assuring me that we were still going in the right direction for St Petra, which was the next village to Poldrissick along the coast.

We found ourselves in a farmyard, were barked at by a savage-looking dog, and turned tail to plough through an overgrown thicket and across a field, traversing what was almost certainly private property.

We emerged at last on a track overgrown with nettles which stung my bare legs and called forth bitter recriminations from me. We were lost, I told him. Hopelessly, hopelessly lost. We would probably spend the rest of our lives wandering round this trackless waste. Simon, who had climbed on a gate, took no notice.

"There's a house," he said. "It's a ruin. It's *super!*"

To children — perhaps to anyone — there is a fascination in such places, and we were no exception. The cottage lay at the foot of a grassy, sloping meadow, with thick woodland forming a multi-textured backdrop behind it. Even from a distance we could tell that it was empty. We raced down the hill towards it, all our differences forgotten.

"It would be a marvellous place to camp," Simon said. "What a terrific hideout it would make!"

I didn't ask who or what we would be hiding from. It was tacitly understood that a refuge from adults was a desirable commodity for any child, particularly Simon. From that moment the cottage became our own, secret place. Was it a refuge still, I wondered? Was that sagging, leaking roof even now providing shelter for Simon?

We learned that the stream which now ran sluggishly alongside the cottage had once been much more turbulent and that a mill had stood there. Later, when this had fallen into disuse, the Trewarthas of Poldrissick Manor had utilised the cottage as a dwelling for their gamekeeper.

In those days the Manor had been a bustling, prosperous place, housing a large family. Great parties had been held there. The lady who came to clean for us at Sea View had a grandmother who had worked there, and she regaled us with stories of the Manor in its heyday.

I had been fascinated by them, particularly as the Manor was by that time empty and deserted, its beautiful grounds néglected. I regarded the place with an awe that was touched by sadness, for to me it had the glamour of Sleeping Beauty's castle.

The cottage was another example of how the estate had gone to rack and ruin. The mill itself had been demolished long before we had arrived on the scene. It seemed likely that by now the cottage would have gone the same way.

We had never actually slept there, but we had fixed up the downstairs room so that it was weather-proof, using wood and branches and old sacks that we found in the wood behind the cottage. One day, Simon had discovered an old car seat on a dump and triumphantly we had dragged it through the fields back to Mill Cottage, as we discovered the place was called, so that we could sit in comfort as we ate the picnic our wondering mother had provided. She seemed surprised that we found so much to occupy ourselves with in the fields all day long, but I imagine was far too glad to get rid of us to ask many questions.

We managed to find a much quicker and easier way to get there, but a certain amount of cross-country walking was still involved. I went back to the main road now and continued uphill, looking for the track. My memory of where exactly it joined the road was imprecise. Was it really this far from the village? It hadn't seemed so far before — or perhaps the onset of old age accounted for that.

I almost missed it, it was so overgrown. The path was wet and muddy, but I had stout shoes on and didn't mind it. The weather was giving me more cause for concern than the ground beneath my feet. Having started reasonably sunny, the sky had clouded over and was now definitely threatening rain. Never mind.

I was so pleased to have found the path we had trodden so often before that nothing now would have stopped me exploring further.

The route came back to me as I walked. There was the farm where we had trespassed that first day, away in the valley to my left. Here was the kissing-gate and the lane — but here there were changes, for where it had been previously little more than an overgrown footpath, now it was wide enough for a car and indeed, tyre-tracks crossing and recrossing told me that it was frequently used.

The five-barred gate was still there, but instead of an expanse of grass broken only by the gorse bushes, now the car track continued all the way down to the cottage. The roof had been renewed and smoke was rising from the chimney. It was no longer derelict but in fact looked delightfully restored as if a great deal of money had been lavished on it.

Twelve years is a long time, I said ruefully to myself. You can't surely be surprised that things have changed? It would have been beyond the realms of possibility to find Simon still using it as his refuge.

And then I saw him, yards away, making his way down the slope towards the cottage from the direction of the wood. He was dressed just as I had seen him on the news bulletin: jeans, sweater, duffle coat. Frantically I yelled and waved.

He stopped dead in his tracks, his face a white blur as he looked towards me. Hurriedly I fumbled at the gate fastening to get into the field and I began running in his direction, the soggy ground sucking at my shoes and causing me to slip and slide.

He was standing stock-still, looking at me — tall and dark and utterly immobile. Dangerously I slithered on the wet grass and for a split second my attention was distracted as I regained my balance, and when I

43

next looked up, he was gone.

From the back of the cottage a dog was barking. He must have gone in, I thought, scanning the field before me. Either that, or he had run back into the woods.

My main emotion was anger. I was furious that he should treat me like this! If he thought I would be content to leave things unresolved, then he had another think coming!

More carefully I scrambled down the hill towards the cottage. There was a small stone bridge now where the track continued across the stream, in place of the stepping-stones we had skipped across as children.

Now that I was nearer I could see that the place had indeed been restored regardless of expense. But, for all that, it was still a hideaway, I thought, as I approached it. It was still hidden from the world until one actually reached that five-barred gate; still set in such a position that no other habitation was visible from any of its windows.

A new but mud-spattered foreign sports car was parked at the back of it and I frowned in bewilderment. Simon didn't go in for friends who owned expensive vehicles like that, still less could he have bought one for himself. At least, I amended, not when I last saw him — and if he could afford one now, then Lynn's theory that he could be involved in some shady deal began to look feasible.

The dog, a shaggy, black and white animal of mixed parentage, stood in the backyard and barked at me, but there was no real malice in him and he frisked round me in a friendly manner as I approached the door. I knocked and waited in vain for a reply. And as I waited, I glanced around where through a side window I could dimly see the figure of a man, tall and dark, standing silently as if waiting for me to leave.

Angrier than every, I banged on the door. This was no polite rat-a-tat, but a furious onslaught on the bright new blue paint and at this I heard footsteps approaching the door, boots clattering noisily on uncarpeted tiles. The door was flung open.

He shouted something, but I didn't hear the words. I realised that I was staring foolishly, and shut my mouth with a gulp of embarrassment.

He was Simon's height and Simon's shape. He had dark hair of the same length and was dressed just as Simon had been dressed when I saw him on the television screen; but to my acute discomfiture I realised that I was looking into the furious face of a stranger.

Though not quite a stranger, I corrected myself, as suddenly I recognised the man who stood before me. That's a face I know as well as my own.

FIVE

"You're Benedict Farrell," I said stupidly.

"I am aware of that fact." His diction was perfect, as always, and his voice loaded with sarcasm. "As I imagine you must have been before you came here battering my door down."

"No — no really, believe me, I'm most dreadfully sorry." I was covered with confusion now I realised the enormity of the mistake I had made. "I had no idea you lived here."

"You're not a reporter?" His tone had mollified slightly, I was thankful to note. Coming face to face with Benedict Farrell was unnerving enough under any circumstances, but being shouted at in that well-known voice made me feel like crawling into a little hole in the ground. I was not, however, too unnerved to wonder what Lynn would say when I told her about it. She admired him more than most — which was saying something. I had seen him on the small screen, the large screen, the West End stage and at Stratford-upon-Avon. He participated with great wit in panel games and was the voice behind more advertisements than I could remember.

"No," I said earnestly. "I'm not a reporter, honestly. I'm sorry to have bothered you. I thought I might find my brother here."

"Why?" he asked.

"It's — rather a long story."

"Do I know him?"

"No." I gestured vaguely at the cottage. "It's just that he used to come here when he wanted to hide. It

46

was just a crazy idea of mine that he might have come back, I see that now."

"Why does he want to hide?"

Why, why, why, I thought irritatedly, just as my mother used to say when we were children.

"It's a long story," I said again.

With that it began to rain, very heavily.

"It looks as if you'd better come in and tell me about it," he said.

I stepped inside the hall, feeling as awkward and ill at ease as I had ever done in the whole of my life. Explanations and apologies were still due from me, I felt.

"You see, you did look like him from a distance," I said. "And I'd talked myself into half expecting to find him here."

"Yes, never mind that." His voice was impatient but not angry any more, for which I was thankful. "I just want to know why. Come on in — take off your coat. It looks as if this rain has set in for a bit. Would you like some coffee?"

"Oh, please don't trouble —"

"No trouble. I was just going to have one myself. Actually," he went on, "I'm not in the least averse to visitors — it's only bloody reporters I can't stand. I'm thinking of getting a shotgun. Old Heinz, the pooch out there, practically lays a red carpet and invites them inside."

He was leading the way into the sitting-room as he spoke and I was delighted to find how beautifully the interior had been restored, making one large room with a stone fireplace at one end. A huge desk surrounded with bookshelves occupied the wall beneath the windows. Glowing Indian rugs were on the polished wood floor. Never in a million years could I have imagined our poor, ramshackle cottage looking like this.

"Do sit down," he said, indicating a comfortable lether chair by the fire. "Sorry the place is in such a mess."

In fact, the mess consisted only of surface clutter — books, magazines, a record sleeve, newspapers. Things that to me simply made it look cosy and lived-in.

The desk was the dominant feature of the room and my gaze rested on it with interest. Much had been written in the popular press concerning the fact that Benedict Farrell had turned his back on his phenomenally successful acting career since the publication of his first novel — a fascinating, spicy, highly readable story of the theatre, which had shot to the top of the bestseller lists on both sides of the Atlantic — and I liked to think that perhaps I was looking at the very desk on which it had been written.

He returned with two mugs of coffee, handed me one and perched on the edge of the desk, regarding me with deep suspicion.

"I've been thinking while I've been in the kitchen," he said. "Your story sounds incredibly thin. Virtually threadbare, in fact. Are you sure you're not a reporter?"

"Positive."

"But what you said about your brother makes no sense at all. This place was a ruin before I bought it. He couldn't have lived here."

"He didn't *live* here. It's just that it was a sort of refuge for us when we were children, and I had this wild idea that he might be using it as a refuge again."

"Is he on the run?"

I hesitated.

"Smuggling, perhaps?" His voice had taken on a new edge of interest and he leaned towards me, his eyes bright with eagerness. It struck me that I had

48

never encountered anyone who brought such energy and passion to being angry or suspicious or just curious. "It still goes on, I'm quite sure of it. The place was noted for it in the past, of course — and wrecking, too, though that's gone out of style, thank heaven. It was a murderous business. But smuggling, now, that has always seemed to me relatively harmless, unless we're talking about drugs. He's not into smuggling heroin, is he? Or illegal immigrants?"

"No, no." Impatiently I brushed such fantasies aside. "It's nothing like that." I spoke as if the truth were more believable but as soon as the words were out of my mouth I realised that if his theories sounded like fiction, the truth put them in the shade. "It's nothing like that," I said again, less forcefully.

"Well, tell me all," he said.

I sighed. Until that point I had told no one in Poldrissick the whole truth, merely saying that my brother had been seen there and had been missing from home for a long time. Now it seemed to me that the most wonderful thing in the world would be to unburden myself to someone else — and who better than this strange but arresting man who asked why, why, why all the time and fixed me with a look that seemed to pulsate with intelligent interest.

"I'm not at all sure that I should. Anyway, you won't take any of it seriously."

"Try me."

It was a relief to recount the whole thing. I began from the moment I had seen the news bulletin until I had hammered on his door.

"You'll say it couldn't possibly have been Simon," I finished. "It's what anyone would say. But Lynn and I both saw him and were both convinced. Go on — tell me we're mad and deluded and guilty of wishful thinking."

He was looking at me with intense concentration.

"No," he said.

"What?"

"I don't think you're mad and deluded. You mentioned that you recognised your brother's walk. Well, any actor knows that the walk is just about the most individual thing about anyone. It's the thing I always work on first — used to work on, I should say — because once you've mastered the walk, you've gone a long way to capturing the essence of the character. Ask any policeman. Many a criminal in disguise has been brought to justice simply because of his walk. It's something that's very hard to change."

I smiled widely at him with relief. It was balm to my spirit to have such enthusiastic support.

"But what can he possibly be doing here? And, more important, where is he now?" I asked.

"Hm." Benedict rubbed his chin and looked at me with narrowed eyes. "He looks like me, you say?"

"No, not a bit. Oh, I know I thought you were like him from a distance, but it was more your shape and colouring and clothes. Simon's face is thinner, with higher cheekbones."

And the difference isn't confined to bone structure, I thought. I had always considered Simon reasonably attractive, but it was the animation in his face that made it so, not his pleasant but unremarkable features.

Benedict Farrell, on the other hand, could never be described as unremarkable. His hair was strong and slightly curly, his skin flushed with the sort of peach bloom that one sees in people born and bred in sunny climates. His eyebrows were two dark, graceful wings over eyes the colour of brown sherry, his nose large but well shaped, his mouth — I forcibly stopped myself from considering his mouth, telling myself that my thoughts were running on like the many

50

adulatory articles I had read about him.

"Also," I said, "he's considerably younger. Only twenty-two."

Benedict grinned.

"A mere stripling. I'm thirty-five."

"I know."

He groaned.

"Everyone knows everything about me. Can you wonder I have this thing about reporters? They have this totally inane preoccupation about my private life, from which actress I last took out to dinner to my taste in breakfast cereals."

Which actress *did* he last take out to dinner? I tried desperately hard to recall what I had read about his love life. Details escaped me. I only knew that his name had been linked with several different women in the past few years, all as glamorous and as well known as he was himself. As if guessing my thoughts, he grinned at me.

"Down here I'm wedded to my work," he said. "But not so wedded that I can't take time out to help a damsel in distress. Especially a damsel as pretty as you. Do you realise you haven't introduced yourself yet?"

I told him my name, at the same time telling myself to beware of all that high-powered charm. He's famous, I cautioned myself. A Personality to whose door newspaper reporters beat a path. This interest, this close attention, the quick, eager, confiding smile that suddenly makes me feel attractive and important are undoubtedly all things that can be switched on and off like a light.

"At least I'm grateful that you haven't laughed me to scorn," I said.

"Do you have a photograph of your brother?"

Once more I produced the picture of Simon. He

51

studied it carefully before handing it back to me.

"I certainly don't remember having seen him. Whereabouts on the quay did he come from when you saw him?"

I described the whole thing in detail.

"So he was walking from the end of the quay towards the village?"

"It's hard to say if he walked from the end of the quay, exactly. I only saw him for a second before he was off the screen — but, yes, he must have come from that direction. Either that or from the little beach beyond the harbour wall."

"Or from a boat."

I stared at him.

"Of course — that's what must have happened. He landed from a boat and came ashore to buy provisions. That means he could be miles away by now."

Benedict frowned thoughtfully biting his lip.

"Cap'n Pengelly should know. He's the harbourmaster — yes, we have one even in little old Poldrissick. It's his job to check vessels in and out. We can at least go and ask him."

"We?" I asked. "Mr Farrell, I don't want to bother you —"

"My dear girl, try keeping me away! This is the most intriguing thing that's come my way for a long time. Far more enthralling than this rubbish." He flicked a dismissive finger at the paper in his typewriter. "And my friends call me Ben, by the way."

"It's not rubbish," I said quickly. "Well, the last one wasn't. I loved it."

"What a charming child you are, to be sure." He smiled at me in a way that made me fully aware that he did not really regard me as a child. "Look, the rain's eased off. Let's go down to the village and find Cap'n Pengelly, shall we? Unfortunately, I don't own a deerstalker hat or yet a magnifying glass, but I can do quite a nice line in creased raincoats. I believe it's what all the best private eyes are wearing this year."

I smiled at this, but only half-heartedly, not ready yet to treat the search for Simon as a vehicle for Benedict Farrell's dramatic talents. He leaned forward and touched my arm.

"Relax," he said. "Don't look so strained. We can achieve just as much with a light touch."

His voice was caressing and it made a slight shiver go down my spine. It always had, I remembered, even when he was doing nothing but extolling the virtues of instant coffee.

"I saw you in *Antony and Cleopatra*," I said.

"Did you enjoy it?"

"I adored it. It's my favourite thing. I heard you saying 'I am dying, Egypt, dying' for weeks afterwards. It haunted my dreams."

"How very uncomfortable for you."

"Won't you miss it?"

"The theatre? Yes, of course I will. But with only one life one's bound to miss something, surely. I was lucky. Success in the theatre came to me pretty quickly, so I've had time to savour it before going on to something else. Now I couldn't live without writing."

I asked him why he had chosen to live in Poldrissick. We were driving towards the village as he explained to me that he had bought the cottage from Jessica Trewartha, who was 'a friend of a friend', and now lived at the Manor.

"It was empty when we were here before."

"It was empty for years. George Trewartha — he was Jessica's husband — inherited it from an old uncle four or five years ago. It was already more or less of a ruin because the uncle had been in a Home for goodness knows how long — eccentric and senile but not

53

certifiable enough for anyone to take over the disposition of his property. The Trewarthas were in Hong Kong at the time of his death and had plans to come home and smarten the place up. However, poor George had a heart attack and died only a few weeks after they arrived in England.

"The poor woman. What did she do?"

"Oh, Jessica has guts, you have to hand it to her. She moved into the old servants' quarters and started doing the place up around her. Mill Cottage was one of the first places she turned her attention to, and it came on the market just as I was looking for a bolt-hole to get away from it all."

"Especially reporters."

"That's right. Since then she's restored the little lodge by the main gate and rents that to a retired colonel and his wife and has converted the Manor into two luxury flats, with another almost finished."

"She sounds quite a lady."

"She has a real flair for that sort of thing. You must meet her."

I made polite noises but in fact I saw little point in meeting Jessica Trewartha. My overwhelming concern was to find Simon, and it seemed unlikely that she would be able to help.

"What's your brother like?" Ben asked suddenly after a few moments' silence.

"You've seen the photograph," I said. "He's about your height —"

"I mean, what's he *really* like? Never mind his vital statistics."

I thought about it.

"He's a bit of a rebel," I said at last. "He gives the impression of wild, feckless youth, but he's not really like that. He knows what he wants out of life."

"Is he the sort to have been led astray?"

"Definitely not. He's a strong character and he's got high principles about honesty. I mean honesty in relationships and the way he sees himself, though he's scrupulous in other ways too. If that makes him sound a prig, he's not, even though I've known him go chasing all over a bus to find the conductor rather than get off without paying."

"Really?" Ben turned to look at me with his eyebrows comically raised. "How strange! It sets me up for the day if I can get the better of London Transport. What did he do — I mean before he threw everything up and went sailing?"

I told him about Simon's succession of labouring jobs and his ambition to write.

"A fellow scribe, eh? All the more reason for us to find him." He was silent for a moment, as if thinking over all that I had told him. "I rather like the sound of him," he said, after a moment.

Inwardly I smiled. He had spoken the words as if he were conferring some sort of accolade — the Benedict Farrell Seal of Approval. But in spite of recognising the arrogance of the man beside me, I was aware of the strangest feeling. It was as if by his very presence he had somehow caused me to shift into a higher gear — as if life had taken on some deeper significance.

Surreptitiously I studied him. There was a glow about him, as if he were more recklessly alive than other people. Wait until I tell Lynn, I thought — not for the first time. She's never going to believe this.

"Well?" he said. "Do I look the same as I do on telly? Don't blush, darling — everyone stares."

"How tedious for you," I said coolly, turning my attention to the countryside, which availed me little since we were driving through a twisting lane with such tall hedges that I could not see over the top of them. "Have we passed the Manor gate yet? I don't remember this at all."

"We're coming up to it now."

There was the greystone lodge, and a gate standing open. The drive, thickly treed on both sides, wound out of sight, and of the Manor itself there was no sign. It was hidden among the trees at the end of the drive.

It took us only a few minutes to arrive at the crossroads where earlier I had turned off to visit Sea View, and from there we rapidly approached Poldrissick. Almost too rapidly. Ben drove with a great deal of dash and speed and I had to school myself not to press imaginary brakes as he swept round the curves and into the square. I felt it was entirely characteristic that he ignored all warning signs and parked his car directly against a yellow line outside the harbourmaster's office.

Cap'n Pengelly was a large, slow-speaking, weather-beaten man with mild blue eyes, and seemed to me a little out of place behind a desk. It looked as if he were used to wider horizons. He wore an official-looking cap with 'Harbour Master' printed on the front of it and he smoked an evil pipe which surrounded his head in a cloud of smoke, the effluvium from which made my eyes water from a distance of six feet. He greeted us in a friendly enough manner and listened carefully to Ben's explanation of our visit, his expression giving nothing away. When I passed him the photograph, he studied it almost as perfunctorily as Jack Watkin had done.

"Never seen him in me life," he said, the smoke that wreathed about him lending an air of inscrutability.

"He was in the village last Sunday," Ben said. "Did any strange vessel arrive during the morning, just about the time the TV people were on the quay?

We thought he might have tied up briefly to buy provisions."

The old seaman shook his head slowly, his eyes resting on me with a strange expression in them.

"If he did, he didn't report to me. You say he's your brother, miss?"

"That's right."

"How many brothers do you have?"

I frowned at him in bewilderment.

"Only one. Why?"

"He's the only son, then?"

"Well, yes — but does that matter?"

"Strange, that."

His voice, while not as heavily accented as many I had heard in the village, held the soft burr of the West Countryman, and he spoke slowly, refusing to be hurried. He sucked at his pipe and continued to regard me with an unreadable expression on his face.

"Why is it strange?" Ben asked, his crisp tones contrasting sharply with Cap'n Pengelly's measured words.

For a moment the old man said nothing, his attention apparently wholly engaged in knocking out his pipe. That done he cocked an eyebrow at me.

"I've a riddle for you," he said at last. "How can an only son have a brother?"

Before I could answer I felt the pressure of Ben's fingers on my arm.

"I take it someone else has been asking about this man," he said.

"Did I say that?"

"In a roundabout way. And this other person also claims to be a brother?"

Cap'n Pengelly was now filling his pipe, pressing the tobacco down with a small metal instrument. If it hadn't been for Ben's restraining hand, I should probably have leapt over the desk and throttled him.

57

"There are times when 'tis hard to determine the truth," he said sententiously.

"Does this young lady look like a liar?" Ben brought all his dramatic talent to bear on the question, but Cap'n Pengelly looked unimpressed.

"I can only tell you what I told the other party," he said. "And goodness knows, he was waving tenners under my nose like he couldn't wait to get rid of them. I've never seen the chap in the photograph, not on that day nor any other."

"This man who waved the tenners," I said. "What was he like?"

The old seaman blew out a cloud of smoke.

"Youngish," he said. "Darkish. Medium sort of height. Medium sort of chap altogether."

"Thank you," I said bitterly. "You've been very helpful."

"Don't take it to heart," Ben said as we strolled round the harbour and came to rest by the wall just beyond the point at which Simon had made his appearance. "The Cornish are inclined to be cagey. They weigh things up before speaking."

"Why do I get the feeling this whole village is ganging up on me? It's infuriating! Why couldn't that wretched man have said from the very beginning that he hadn't seen Simon but that some other man, also purporting to be a brother, had been asking questions? He could have given us that information in two minutes flat instead of going all round the houses, with his riddles and his innuendoes."

"It's the Celt in them," Ben said. "They like to make a drama out of things — extract the last drop of suspense out of a story."

"Who could have been looking for Simon?"

"Well, not the police, that's for sure. They wouldn't wave tenners about. More likely a partner in crime

58

who feels that Simon has ratted on him.

"Oh!" I turned on him angrily. "I do wish you'd believe that Simon hasn't done anything wrong. Whatever the explanation, it isn't that."

"Then maybe you should go to the police."

I made no reply to this but stood silently, staring miserably at two gulls on the shingly little beach fighting shrilly over a piece of offal.

"You're not *that* sure, are you?" Ben persisted.

"I don't know what to think."

"What do we really know?" Ben said thoughtfully after a moment. "We know that somehow he survived the explosion and found his way here. We know that for some unfathomable reason he kept the fact of his survival a secret from his nearest and dearest. We know that somebody else is also looking for him."

"I can't explain any of that – but I'm sure there are people in this village who know more than they're telling."

"That's not something we know for sure."

"Perhaps not. But I have a strong feeling about it."

"It's facts I'm trying to pin down at the moment."

"What about the fact that Cap'n Pengelly doesn't know of a boat arriving that morning? Does that mean there wasn't one, or simply that nobody reported to him?"

"Either. I tend to support the latter, though, because where else did Simon come from, if not the end of the quay? The only other approach he could have made is from here, this beach, and you can see for yourself that's hardly likely."

Waves were pounding against the rocks – steep, high rocks, slippery with sea weed.

"We climbed over there once," I said, memory once more returning to me. "Isn't there a beach beyond?"

"A tiny one – but you can't get in or out of it

59

except at exceptionally low tides. The locals avoid it. Too many people have been cut off there over the years. The cliffs are so steep at that point that there's no way out of it, if anyone should get caught."

"I don't know what to think," I said again.

"It occurs to me that if this other so-called brother has been making inquiries of Cap'n Pengelly, he could have been questioning other people too. Like Jack Watkin."

"Which would account for the fact that he's watchful and suspicious of me!"

"Well, it could. You are quite sure you haven't another brother secreted away somewhere —"

I laughed at him.

"Of course not. Only a brother-in-law, and he —" I stopped suddenly in mid-sentence. "And he's an ex-brother-in-law," I finished slowly. I turned to face Ben. "I wonder. I just wonder. The first two men Simon went sailing with were friends of his, and for some reason Max was very much against him going with them. I said at the time that perhaps he knew something about them that Simon didn't. Could there possibly be any connection?"

Ben looked at me for a moment without speaking. I could tell from his expression that his thoughts were racing.

"I could easily write a scenario to fit," he said.

SIX

"Tell me about this ex-brother-in-law of yours," he said, as we sat in a corner of the Anchor Inn enjoying one of Mrs Watkin's pasties. "Why is he ex? Did he and your sister part amicably? Did she meet somebody else?"

"No, nothing like that."

I fell silent, knowing that if I began to describe Max as he had always appeared to me, Ben would immediately assume that, for reasons of my own, I was exaggerating the catastrophic effect he had had on Lynn. He would think that I was partisan in my championship of Lynn's cause. Besides, I could not think of the words to describe exactly the totally self-centred, scornful, pretentious, opinionated man that the young and handsome Maxwell Thurston had become.

"He's not very nice," I said weakly. "He treated Lynn abominably."

"Like what?"

"He put her down all the time. Over the years, I saw her disintegrate before my eyes." I shrugged. "I disliked the man intensely, I have to admit it, and my opinion is hardly impartial."

Ben was watching me closely as I spoke, his eyes attentive, and once again I was struck with the quality of his concentration. It was as if, at that moment, no one else existed.

"Added to all of that," I went on, "Lynn told me that his business methods are a bit suspect. That's why she was anxious to keep the police out of this until we found Simon and had the chance to talk to him."

"So she thought Max could have had something to do with Simon's disappearance?"

'I don't know what she thought. As I keep saying, Simon had left those friends of Max's a full week before the explosion."

"And joined up with the two North Sea divers. Yes, you told me. Did he simply meet them casually?"

"Apparently so. He decided that he and the other two were incompatible and happened to meet this other couple in a café in Marseilles. Evidently they hit it off right away, so Simon joined up with them. We met their families. They seemed nice, ordinary, pleasant people. One of them was supposed to be getting married in the autumn."

Ben thought this over in silence for a moment.

"How's this, then," he said. "Simon found out something about the other two — say they were involved in drug-running, for example. Maybe that's why he left them in Marseilles — perhaps he didn't want any part of it. Maybe the explosion in Cannes harbour was an accident, maybe it wasn't. Either way, the other two would have been relieved that Simon was removed from the scene. However, six months later they discover that he didn't die after all, so naturally they're worried. He could still talk."

"But if that's so," I said after a moment's thought, "why didn't Simon go at once to the police?"

"Was Lynn still married to Max at the time? If he had any reason to think that Max was involved, he could have kept quiet out of consideration for Lynn."

I frowned as I followed his argument, then laughed.

"We don't even know if it *is* Max who's been asking about Simon, still less that he was anything more than casually friendly with the two men that Simon went sailing with. I think your talent for writing fiction is running away with you."

"Well, you can soon prove the first part."

Jack Watkin was approaching our table, clearing away empty glasses. Ben engaged him in conversation about fishing, flattered him outrageously about his skills, told him a very funny joke and at the end of it all managed to extract quite painlessly the information that we had been seeking. A man purporting to be yet another brother had been asking questions.

"I wish you'd told me," I said, somewhat reproachfully.

"Least said, soonest mended," Jack said succinctly, bending to remove an ashtray. "Us don't care for folks as ask questions."

"Was this man about thirty?" I asked. "Dark and rather good-looking, with a moustache?"

"Sounds like un," Jack admitted. He edged his way around the table to move away from us, but looked back for a parting shot. "'E drove a Porsche," he said. "Metallic blue. Fred Penhaligon gave un a parking ticket."

"That settles it," I said after he had gone. "Max drives a blue Porsche. It has to be him."

"I suppose," Ben said, "he couldn't simply have been concerned for Simon, the way you are yourself? If he saw the news bulletin and recognised him he might just be checking up to ensure that it really was Simon before mentioning the matter to you or your sister. He might want to make absolutely certain of Simon's existence before raising your hopes."

"Max never had any concern for anyone but himself in his whole life," I said savagely. "If he's looking for Simon, then it's for some purpose of his own."

"All right, then." Ben's eyes gleamed, as if having got that point out of the way he could now concen-

63

trate on working out the puzzle in a more dramatic manner. "Max wants Simon because *he* knows that *Simon* knows something to his disadvantage. Like the fact that he and his two friends are engaged in smuggling. Maybe he arranged for the accident in Cannes."

"I suppose – I suppose that would explain why Max didn't want Simon to go with them in the first place. He would know Simon wouldn't involve himself with anything outside the law." I spoke calmly as if Ben's assumption was the most reasonable thing on earth before the enormity of its implications struck me. "Oh, Ben," I said. "That surely has to be nonsense! You're saying that Max is a murderer, as well as a smuggler. And, in any case, how did Simon get from Cannes to Poldrissick and where is he now? And, most of all, why hasn't he told us that he's alive?"

Ben grinned at me.

"I'll have to work on that a bit longer," he said. He leaned across and covered my hand with his. "Look, don't be cross, but I'm going to leave you now. I simply have to put in a few hours work today, come hell or high water – but I'll be in touch, I promise. You will forgive me for dashing off, won't you?"

"Well, of course! You've already spent hours on my problems and I couldn't be more grateful."

I meant what I said, but nevertheless after he had gone I felt bereft, like a fledgling chick pushed out of the nest.

There was, I told myself, absolutely no justification for feeling so abandoned. He had devoted his entire morning to me – a morning which he would no doubt otherwise have spent at his desk producing the next bestseller. Who was I, a perfect stranger, to come between him and his writing? I had, after all, known him for less than three hours. It was just that — well, he'd taken charge of me, somehow, in a way that made me feel I had known him for months rather than hours.

So, how should I spend the afternoon? There was a weak and watery sun shining now which tempted me to walk again along the arm of the harbour, past the wall where the nets were drying, past the seat and the lobster-pots, past the spot where the interview had been filmed. I stood for a moment and considered the scene. Simon *must* have arrived by boat, in spite of the harbourmaster's lack of knowledge of him. There was no other way.

I walked on a little further, back to the wall where Ben and I had leaned and talked just a little while before. The stones on the little beach glistened with the water left by the receding tide. The waves were not now pounding against the rocks, which rose high and dry surrounded by a small apron of sand.

"You're not thinking of taking a dip, are you?" asked a voice behind me. I turned to see Laurie Barron standing and smiling at me. He was dressed in a high-necked black sweater and a rust-coloured canvas smock. 'Macho' was the word, I thought. I smiled back at him.

"Not likely. It takes more than one ray of sunshine to tempt me. I imagine that water's close to freezing."

"True enough."

He came and leaned on the wall beside me.

"Have you remembered where you saw my brother?" I asked him.

"Oh, oh!" He lifted his hands to heaven in mock despair. "I come to chat you up, and before I can open my mouth you're asking more questions —"

"And I'm not the only one, am I? Someone's been here before me, asking the same sort of questions."

65

"You don't say so." He was grinning at me side-ways, and this time it was my turn to look despairing.

"Look, this is serious," I said. "My brother could be in danger."

I don't know why I said it. It was not something that I had been consciously aware of. Max was a man whom I disliked, but even so I had not thought of him as presenting a serious menace. His interest in Simon's whereabouts was apparently inexplicable, but I had not thought of it as a threat. Now I realised that unwittingly I had spoken the truth. Simon could be in danger, if even a half of Ben's suppositions were true.

Laurie was looking at me curiously, not smiling now.

"We don't like people asking questions here," he said.

"That much is obvious."

"What's he supposed to be doing here?"

"You asked me that before." I turned to face him. "I beg you to tell me what you know!"

He was silent for a moment as if considering his words.

"It's little enough," he said at last. "I've seen him, that's all."

"But where?"

He nodded his head towards the rocks and the cliffs beyond.

"Along the cliff, one night — oh, around a month ago, it must have been. He must have been standing there, watching me, hidden in the gorse. I heard him sneeze, shone a torch, and there he was. I asked him what the hell he thought he was doing, just standing there, hiding himself."

"What did he say?"

"He just looked at me and laughed. 'No offence,

mate,' he said. 'You mind your business, I'll mind mine.' "

"And then, what?"

"He just melted away into the darkness. I tried to follow him, but I couldn't see hide nor hair of him."

"Why should you care? Why follow him?"

"Look, he was a stranger — he was spying —"

"On what?"

Laurie smiled again.

"We have simple pleasures in these parts, Miss Kendall. No night clubs, no discos to take your girl to. Just the cliffs and the moon on the water. You really ought to let me show you some time."

I ignored this — hardly registered the words, in fact.

"And you've never seen him since?" I asked.

"Not once. Which perhaps is just as well, for his sake. We don't take too kindly to Peeping Toms."

The idea of Simon in such a role was so ridiculous that I laughed.

"All right," Laurie said. "If it's so amusing, then he must have had some other reason for being there. He wouldn't be a cop, by any chance?"

"Not by any chance."

"Then I'm as baffled as you are."

We leaned on the wall and stared at the sea in silence for a while. My gaze travelled up to the high cliffs, down again to the beach.

"There's a tiny cove beyond these rocks, isn't there?" I said. "What's beyond that?"

"Another cove, and then another. People steer clear of the coast just here as the beaches are all but inaccessible. The cliffs are so sheer that anyone cut off by the tide has no chance at all."

"That's right," I said. "I remember now. When we stayed here before, a boy got into difficulties. They

67

had to bring in the helicopter from Culdrose."

"Hardly a year passes without some fool of a tourist getting into trouble — but the locals know better."

I pointed to the rocks.

"It's possible to get round at low tide, though," I said.

"Anyone'd be a fool to try it, except at spring tide."

"Which is when?"

"New moon and full moon."

I tried to remember what stage in the month we had reached. The moon had been obscured by clouds for the past few nights and in fact it seemed ages since I had seen it at all.

"Mind you," he went on, "with me you'd be safe. I'll take you now, if you like. We've got a clear forty minutes, at a guess, before being cut off — and what, after all, could be more romantic than dying together?"

"I think not, thank you all the same."

"How about living together, then?"

"I'm afraid I have to decline that offer, too."

He laughed at that, not at all put out that I appeared less than bowled over by his charms. I had the feeling that the coming summer would provide a succession of far more susceptible females for his entertainment.

"Oh, well," he said, smiling whitely at me. "You win some, you lose some. I'll bear up the best I can."

"I'm sure you will!" Indeed, I was certain of it. His mildly flirtatious approach seemed mechanical to me. He simply had no idea how else to talk to a woman. "Tell me," I went on, "are there any houses along the cliff in these coves you mention?" Try as I might, I could not remember anything about them although I knew that Simon and I had explored them in the past.

"All the land belongs to the Manor," he said. "You can see it from the cliffs. There's nothing else, though."

"Oh, yes, of course! But there's a cottage, isn't there? A little house, halfway down the cliff?"

"Cottage?" Laurie looked at me in bewilderment. "No — oh!" His brow cleared. "You mean the Folly. That belongs to the Manor too, but you can hardly call it a cottage. It's more of a summerhouse. I heard that Mrs Trewartha was thinking of renovating it along with the rest of the property, but she gave up the idea. There's no road of access, no services, no way down to the cove."

He could be there, I thought. He could be hiding out, camping in the Folly. I hardly noticed Laurie pushing himself away from the wall, saying that he would have to go, that he had work to do. I called after him when he had gone a few yards.

"Wait a second! When's full moon?"

He turned and laughed at me.

"Having second thoughts? You want to see the moon on the water? You'll have to wait three weeks . . ."

So it was full, or as near as makes no difference, a week before. The tide would have been at its lowest then, and Simon could have walked round the rocks from the direction of those all but inaccessible coves and the cliffs where Laurie had seen him that night.

I looked again at the fringe of sand around the end of the rocks. Forty minutes, Laurie had said. If I allowed myself half that amount of time, I would at least be able to see the lie of the land; would, perhaps, be able to assess if my theory was remotely possible.

I checked my watch. It was ten minutes to three. I made a resolution to keep a careful eye upon the time, climbed down to the beach and clambered round the rocks.

I was glad that I had done so. The beach was sandier here, the waves more gentle, surging and retreating in small curls that left a trail of bubbles

69

behind them. There was a smell of salt and seaweed in the air. I picked up a flat stone and sent it skimming over the waves.

I was completely out of sight of the harbour even though it was still very near. Sheer cliffs towered above me to the scudding clouds. A cormorant took off from a high ledge, and always there was the shriek of gulls.

Swiftly I walked across the beach to the rocks which marked the boundary of the cove. I looked at my watch. Time was running short, but I could go on a little further.

Here it was necessary to climb, negotiating small pools full of sea-urchins and tiny, darting fish. Once over the rocks I found myself in a smaller, enclosed inlet. On the shore side, high above me, was Poldrissick Manor, surrounded by trees but commanding an uninterrupted view of the sea. On the cliff which marked the far side of the cove stood the building which Laurie had referred to as the Folly. It clung to the cliff as if only determination kept it from falling. Who built it, I wondered? Some dead and gone Trewartha, no doubt, who liked to watch the sea in solitude. An artist, perhaps, or a birdwatcher. If there was a path down to it, it was hidden from me, and certainly the climb from the Folly to the beach was a difficult one. But not impossible. Not for someone as young and fit as Simon.

Heavens, the time! I turned to leave, but as I did so the sun came out and at the same time a glint of light flashing from the direction of the Folly caught my eye. I looked, but could see nothing. Then the flash came again and with it a slight movement. Someone was there, pressed against the side of the small building. The light was coming from a reflection of the sun on a glass lens. Whoever the watcher might be, he had binoculars trained on me. The realisation caused an unpleasant trickle of distaste to run down my spine, even though it reinforced my view that this could be Simon's refuge.

Whoever it might be, I had no time to waste in speculation. I had to begin my return journey without delay if I were to avoid being cut off by the tide — a prospect which was even more unappealing now that I had refreshed my memory concerning the height of those cliffs.

I made it without difficulty, which made me more convinced than ever that Simon could have walked to the village and back, given an exceptionally low tide. But if he were the watcher up at the Folly, why had he not shown himself to me? Nothing made sense. Ben's theory, that he had arrived by boat, was far more likely — and yet Laurie had seen him on the cliffs, a month ago. Watching and waiting.

I bought myself a cup of tea in a café by the harbourside and wandered rather aimlessly back to my room at the Anchor, uncertain what to do next. It was cold and cheerless, and suddenly I felt more depressed than I had done since this business began. For heaven's *sake*, I told myself. Simon's alive — that's all that matters, really. I tried to convince myself that he had good reason for keeping hidden, that, above all, I had to trust him. But I still felt depressed.

I wish I could talk to Ben, I thought. I've got quite a bit to tell him. The fact that Laurie Barron had admitted seeing him on the cliff, for one thing, and my theory about the Folly for another. I thought of phoning him, and I found the thought dangerously attractive.

There's no reason why you shouldn't, one half of me argued. After all, it's a new development. He'd be

71

interested that I'd proved to my satisfaction that Simon could have reached the quay from the beach.

But you can't interrupt if he's working, the other half of me said. Just imagine his fury! I'd seen him angry once, and the last thing on earth I wanted was to incur his wrath again. A telephone line would no doubt be unnecessary — I would be able to hear that crisp, perfect diction delivering its blistering attack quite unaided by technology.

On the other hand, he had said that the whole question of Simon's whereabouts was intriguing and enthralling. Those were his very words. In those circumstances, perhaps he wouldn't mind . . .

I felt unsure of myself in a way I thought I had long outgrown. My longing to renew the contact between myself and Ben surprised me by its intensity. You're a fool, I told myself. An impressionable, idiotic woman who has suddenly started behaving like a star-struck teenager. Yet when I remembered the warm sympathy in his attentive eyes, common sense deserted me. I wanted to see him again, and there was no way I could talk myself out of that.

Should I ring him? I was still debating the question when a knock sounded on my door and Mrs Watkin stuck her head into the room to tell me that I was wanted downstairs.

It was Ben.

"Wretched woman," he greeted me, smiling. "You've stopped me working all afternoon, and there's a sea of crumpled paper all around my desk to prove it."

I was so happy to see him. I had been upstairs in that sterile room for less than half an hour on my own but for some reason it seemed like days of solitary confinement, and I was careless of the fact that my joy was there for him to see.

72

"Get your coat," he said. "Let's go back to my place." He raised his voice so that Mrs Watkin lurking somewhere out of sight, could hear him. "Sarah won't be in to dinner, Mrs Watkin!" he called.

"Won't I?" I asked.

"I have plans for us."

He put his hand through my arm and led me over to his car, which he had parked in the square with a fine disregard of notices, yellow lines, or anything else.

"You get away with murder," I remarked.

"Don't I, though? One needs panache, of course."

Which he had in abundance, there was no doubt of that.

I wasted no time in telling him of Laurie Barron's revelation about having seen Simon lurking on the cliff one night.

"Lurking?" Ben repeated, with an amused lift of his eyebrow.

"That's what he said. Trying to keep out of sight, anyway."

"He's done that pretty successfully for six months, hasn't he?"

"Ben, what about the Folly? Could he be living there?"

He thought about it, frowning.

"It's secluded enough, heaven knows. I went there once with Jessica when she was contemplating turning it into a holiday cottage, and we actually saw the tide rushing in. It was one of the things that made her decide not to bother with it. One could imagine the unwary holidaymaker being swept away in no time flat. Which reminds me —"

He kept his eyes on the road but stretched out his left hand to touch me. "What the hell do you think you were doing, going round there? I don't care what Laurie Barron said. It was a risk you should never

73

have taken."

"At least I proved that Simon could have climbed down from the Folly and walked to the village and back."

"Is he a climber? He'd need to be."

"I wouldn't call him an expert, but he's done a bit."

Ben was shaking his head as I spoke.

"I can't imagine he'd be living there. Jessica would have mentioned it."

"Perhaps she doesn't know. Someone was there, Ben, looking at me through binoculars. A singularly unpleasant feeling, if I may say so."

"That could have been a birdwatcher, or someone keeping an eye on passing ships."

"Or Simon," I added hopefully.

"Or Max."

I looked at him in horror at this.

"Oh, no! What a ghastly thought."

We had arrived at the Mill Cottage by this time and were sitting by a log fire. After my room at the Anchor, I felt that I had reached a veritable haven of warmth and comfort. Even so, the thought that Max could have been watching me from the cliff made me shiver.

"I've been thinking about this Max of yours," Ben said. "He's obviously a day or two ahead of you. I can't help wondering if his inquiries have been any more successful than ours. If he has an unlimited supply of ten-pound notes, they just might have been."

"I don't think Laurie said anything."

"Did he say so?"

"No — it was simply an impression I got. It seemed that he was reluctant to talk about seeing Simon on the cliff, as if he had something to hide. Maybe he was with someone else's wife."

"Knowing Laurie Barron, that wouldn't be outside

74

the realms of possibility. Max could have found someone to give him information — someone we haven't managed to dig up. And if he has, Sarah, you do realise that Simon could be in danger? It may sound melodramatic to assume that Max was responsible for the so-called accident in Cannes, but it's a distinct possibility if he and his two friends were involved in something shady together — something that Simon discovered. He could have threatened to turn them in."

"I'd thought of that," I said. "And I'd also thought that Simon probably has no idea at all that anyone knows that he's still alive. He might well be totally unaware that he was caught by the TV camera. So he'd never suspect that anyone is looking for him. He wouldn't be on his guard against Max."

Ben leaned back in his chair, frowning at the ceiling.

"Everything hinges on whether there was any unlawful sort of connection between Max and the two men Simon went sailing with. If he was only a casual acquaintance, then my theory falls to the ground."

"There's no way we can prove that, one way or the other," I said despairingly. "I don't even know their names, and nor does Lynn."

"Perhaps the Secretary of the Sailing Club would know."

He transferred his gaze to me, his voice suddenly becoming excited.

"I suppose he might," I agreed doubtfully.

"I could phone him — give him some spiel about finding out background information for a book — tell him I'd like to contact the two men . . ." His voice trailed away as I signally failed to become equally enthusiastic.

"It was so long ago," I said. "And there are so many boats. Still, I suppose it's worth a try."

"People do tend to co-operate when I tell them who I am," Ben said diffidently.

"Yes," I agreed. "I expect they do."

"The thought appears to depress you!"

I denied that absolutely, yet he was not far from the truth. Sitting there in close proximity to him by the fireside, I longed suddenly for him to be ordinary and unfamous. As it was, I felt certain that he regarded my incursion into his life as intriguing entertainment, nothing more. Once the puzzle was solved, once we had discovered — or not discovered — just where and why Simon was hiding himself, he would forget me and return to the glamorous women of the society columns, of that I felt sure.

"You could try the club," I said, more to change the current of my thoughts than because I had any real hope that it would be of use. "Why not?"

Directory Inquiries gave him the number of the club and he was through to the Secretary very quickly. He identified himself and made his inquiries, which to me sounded totally convincing — however, as I had feared, we learned nothing.

"A very kind gentleman," Ben said, as he replaced the receiver. "Full of advice about books that would give me all the information I need, but with absolutely no idea about the two men who went sailing with Max Thurston's brother-in-law. He did proffer the information that he hadn't seen Max for some time, however."

Which got us nowhere. Silence settled upon us as Ben seemed lost in thought. Finally he slapped his knee.

"This is silly," he said. "We have no way of establishing whether or not Max had any connection with those men, so we must concentrate on this end. We'll go and see Jessica and ask her if she's seen Simon anywhere on her property. I swear she'll know if by any chance he has been camping in the Folly. There's not much that escapes her eye."

"She sounds just the slightest bit formidable," I said, as we drove to the Manor. "What sort of age is she?"

"Jessica?" Ben laughed. "I'd hate to guess. I imagine she must be over fifty, but you'd never know it. She was a beautiful woman — is still a beautiful woman, though I imagine that these days it takes a little longer."

He was silent for a moment as he manoeuvred the car around several potholes in the lane.

"She seemed a poor, pathetic little thing when she was first widowed," he went on, "but she's rallied remarkably well. I think she forced herself into doing all this work on the estate so that she didn't have time to brood too much. She's a social sort of creature and goes away to stay with friends in London quite frequently, but underneath I think she's lonely and terrified of growing old in a way that perhaps only a beautiful woman can be. I suppose when a woman has traded on her looks all her life it's bound to be traumatic when they begin to fade."

"I suppose it must be," I agreed. "It's a fate I'll be spared, anyway."

"Rubbish!" His voice was casual. "Such self-abasement is quite unnecessary. You have a very nice little face."

I laughed.

"My goodness," I said. "You overwhelm me!"

Theatrically Ben sighed.

"Why women set such store by looks I shall never understand. Most beautiful women make it a full-time job just staying that way. You, on the other hand, are quite as good looking as any woman needs

77

to be and yet not so good looking that you can afford to neglect the rest of you. Believe me, I've mixed with more beautiful women in the acting profession than you've had hot dinners, but on the whole your company is preferable to most of them."

"You're too kind." The touch of arrogance amused me but in no way spoiled the pleasure I extracted from the compliment, if compliment it could be called.

"Besides," he went on. "Looks don't really have a lot to do with sexiness, do they? I mean, look at Edith Piaf — she was as sexy as all-get-out, but her best friend couldn't call her pretty. Now, Jessica for some reason leaves me totally cold, and I don't simply mean because she's considerably older than I am. Age is another thing that really has nothing to do with it."

"Can I quote you on all of this?" I asked, smiling at him. "Benedict Farrell's views on women might be quite a saleable proposition."

"If I didn't trust you, I wouldn't talk," he said.

Now that, I thought, really *was* a compliment, and I treasured it accordingly.

We had by this time reached the lodge gates, and we both fell silent. I had no way of guessing at Ben's thoughts. I suddenly felt happier than for some time past simply because I was with him and he was steadfastly on my side, apparently determined to see this thing through with me.

The drive was long and on each side of it loomed trees and shrubs. The headlights gleamed on the leaves of rhododendrons and laurels, the slight mist that had come with evening diffusing the light so that outlines were blurred and softened.

The house was out of sight, but then the drive curved and the trees thinned, and there before us was the Manor, grey and solid, with two wings spreading

78

from the central steps. Two stone lions crouched on either side of the massive door.

"That's all divided into four," Ben said. "We go round to the back for Jessica's part of the house."

We parked in a courtyard. It was a large paved area, the flagstones shining palely in the light of an old-fashioned street lamp. Across the yard was a long building with a clock tower that struck seven as we stood there.

"Those were the stables," Ben said. "I think Jessica intends turning her attention to those now that the last of the flats is finished."

He led me to a white-painted door set in the dark stone of the main house. Spring flowers grew in profusion in window-boxes on either side of it, and beside it hung an old-fashioned bell-pull. Ben tugged it forcefully and we heard the bell jangling inside the house.

The door was flung open. Even with the build-up that Ben had given her, I was surprised by Jessica Trewartha's looks. Her skin was like porcelain, her hair an attractive silver-gilt and cut in a feathery style which flattered her elfin face. She was made up with care, though her clothes were casual. She wore a black sweater over tight pink pants, and she had the figure of a girl. She gave a cry of delight when she saw Ben.

"My dear, how *lovely*!" she said. "I simply couldn't be more delighted to see you! The west wing is actually finished at last and I was dying for someone to celebrate with."

"I'm your man," Ben said. "Or rather, we're your men. Jessica, this is Sarah — Sarah, this is Jessica. Lead on to the champers, darling."

Jessica smiled at me.

"I'm always pleased to see Ben's friends — bless

him, he always brings them up to see me and I must say that I like nothing better. I mean, one does rather *moulder* here theatre-wise and one misses the bright lights however much one loves the country." She led us through to a charmingly furnished sitting-room and turned to study me. "I can't say I actually know your face, but I'm sure that's merely my ignorance," she said.

"Actually, I —"

"I expect I'm being frightfully, frightfully tactless! You're probably resting and simply don't want to hear the very *word* 'theatre' — well, all right, we'll talk of anything *but*! Ben dear, there does actually happen to be a bottle of bubbly in the fridge — go and do the honours, there's a darling. Sarah, do sit down and tell me everything you've been doing. I hope Ben has been showing you our lovely, lovely countryside —"

Ben left the room with a grin in my direction. He had, I felt, not told me the half about Jessica Trewartha, but in spite of the girlish gush it was impossible not to like her. She was warm and spontaneous and seemed slightly amused at herself — and added to that, she was so very, very pretty.

"What a lovely room," I said.

"Oh, do you like it? It was once the servant's hall, or at least part of it. Such good proportions, don't you think? I needed a big room to set off my Chinese carpets. I brought them home from Hong Kong, you see — and the porcelain, of course. We lived there for fifteen years."

"It must have been fascinating."

"Oh, it was. My husband was the Commissioner of Police and we had a *fabulous* time socially, of course — a far cry from Poldrissick, I can tell you! Ah, here comes Ben. What I should do without him as

80

a neighbour, I really cannot tell you. Here's to my lovely new flat."

Ben raised his glass.

"God bless her and all who sail in her," he said. "May all your tenants have muted hi-fis and wear bedroom slippers."

Jessica laughed.

"The walls are thick and so are the carpets. You really must see the place, Ben — I'm rather proud of this one. There was a time when I thought it would never be finished. The whole thing seems to have been going on and *on* so — I had to wait weeks for the kitchen units and then they delivered the wrong sort. And then the central heating people went on strike. I began to think the whole enterprise was doomed."

"And now it's really finished?"

"Completely. It's furnished too, down to the last ashtray and wastepaper basket."

"Do you have tenants for it?" I asked.

"Not yet, but a perfectly sweet little man is coming to have a look at it tomorrow. He works in the Middle East — a friend of the Westonbirts, who live in the Lodge — but he wants a base here. He sounds ideal. Mm! Lovely, lovely champers. Ben darling, do pour a little more — it's what I call a *manny* sort of a job, pouring drinks, don't you agree, Sarah? Ben it's ages since you came to see me, but then I expect you've been busy-busy-busy." She fluttered her fingers in the air as she spoke, miming intense activity. "I'm so glad you came tonight, and glad you brought Sarah."

She smiled at me brilliantly over the rim of her glass.

"Ben usually brings his visitors to see me," she said. "I adore company. Can't get enough of it."

81

"I'm not exactly staying with Ben," I said hastily, feeling that it was time I made my position clear. "In fact I didn't meet him until this morning." This morning? For a moment I hesitated. It seemed incredible that I had not known him for much longer.

"Really?" Jessica looked puzzled.

"Sarah came to the cottage because she thought her brother might be there. It was once their hide-out when they were kids, staying in the village. Needless to say, he wasn't, but I was. We thought you might be able to offer some helpful suggestions about finding him. Show Jessica the photograph, Sarah."

Once again I withdrew the picture from my hand-bag and passed it over to Jessica. She peered at it shortsightedly, rose with it in her hand and went over to a desk by the window from which she took a pair of spectacles. She stood with her back half turned towards me as she studied it and for a long moment she said nothing. Ben went on explaining, telling Jessica the whole story, including the fact that Laurie Barron had recognised the photograph as the man he had seen on the cliff. He finished speaking and there was silence.

"What a fanciful sort of tale," Jessica said at last, handing the photograph back to me. "Are you sure you haven't been watching too many late-night movies, Sarah?"

She wasn't friendly any more. Until that moment she had been bright and kittenish, bent on charming me just as much as Ben, or so it had seemed. Now her blue eyes were cold and she was no longer smiling. I was aware of little lines around her mouth that I had not noticed before.

"I suppose it must seem like the purest fiction," I agreed. "But Ben told it exactly like it is."

"I can't imagine why you should think I could

throw any light on the matter."

"It was because of the Folly," I said. "We thought — that is, I thought — it seemed the only place where Simon might have been camping, given that he appeared from that direction. Either that, or he could have come from a boat but Cap'n Pengelly says no strange vessel came into harbour that day . . ." I knew that I was becoming more and more incoherent as her gaze dwelt on me, ever more frosty. I looked appealingly at Ben, silently begging for his support.

"Could he have holed up in the Folly, Jessica?" he asked.

She gave a brittle laugh and moved across the room to the fireplace.

"It's a preposterous suggestion," she said, looking at herself in the mirror over the mantelpiece and pushing her hair about as if the matter was too foolish and trivial to merit her full attention. "I'm surprised you entertained the idea for a moment, Ben. You saw the state of it that time we went to look at it. It's practically falling to pieces and, anyway, there's no way down to the beach. It's quite impractical to think your brother could have climbed down and walked to the village, Sarah." She turned from the mirror and looked at me. "Quite impractical," she repeated coldly.

"He might have been there without your knowledge, perhaps," I suggested.

"Never! I walk the dogs every day along that stretch of the cliffs."

"Someone was there today," I said. "Someone was watching me through binoculars."

"An ornithologist, no doubt."

"Well, perhaps . . ." I looked across at Ben, who raised an eyebrow at me. For some reason our questions had antagonised Jessica. Was it because she

83

felt foolish having leapt to the conclusion that I was an actress friend from Ben's theatrical past? Somehow that hardly seemed sufficient reason for such a dramatic change in her manner. Ben stood up.

"Jessica, we must be off," he said. "I thought I'd take Sarah to the Lobster Pot for dinner."

"What a good idea." Jessica smiled at him as if she were making an effort to return to her former good-humoured state. "I'm sure you'll enjoy it. The food's always marvellous. I hope you've booked — it's often hard to get a table."

"I'm afraid I haven't," Ben said. "But they're always terribly good to me, I find, and usually manage to squeeze me in."

I smiled a little at that. In a way, I thought, if I weren't quite so hungry, it might be quite entertaining to be turned away from the restaurant, simply to *show* Benedict Farrell; yet I knew it would never happen. I could recognise the arrogance and be sardonically amused by it, but equally I could understand the warmth and affection he seemed to inspire. It wasn't only his celebrity status, though, admittedly, that helped.

Jessica, although her manner had thawed slightly, made no effort to persuade us to stay. I thanked her for her hospitality and made for the car, thinking that Ben was close behind me, but with my hand on the door I saw that he had been restrained by Jessica, who had a hand on his arm and was talking to him, quickly and earnestly.

"What was all that about?" I asked as he joined me and we drove out of the courtyard.

He looked at me and laughed.

"Jessica doesn't believe your — quote — cock-and-bull story — unquote. She thinks you're a journalist and all this is a clever ruse to get close to me."

"And she accuses me of having an overheated imagination!"

"Oh, I don't know. She could be right."

"Ben, you know she's not!"

He reached out and took my hand.

"Of course I do," he said. "After all, you didn't invent Max in his metallic blue Porsche, did you? We have Jack Watkin's word that he's been asking questions too."

I breathed a sigh of relief.

"I never thought I'd be thankful for Max. Ben, why did Jessica get so uptight about it all? I wasn't accusing her of anything. But from the moment I produced the photograph she seemed almost angry, as if I was trying to make her responsible in some way. One moment she was being all charming and skittish, fluttering her eyelashes at you and being all-girls-together with me, then suddenly we were *persona non grata*. Or I was, at least."

"She's volatile by nature," Ben said. "Her moods are inclined to switch from one extreme to another. I don't honestly think she was angry."

"No? Well, you could have fooled me! Still, I suppose you know her pretty well by this time."

"Yes, I do. I know her very well." Ben's voice was thoughtful. "I've seen her through all sorts of moods since she came here, ranging from despair to elation."

"Well, what's your explanation?"

He waited for a moment before he answered.

"I don't honestly know," he said. "There's a lot more to Jessica than meets the eye. She's not the empty-headed, twittering person she first appears."

"So what changed her so suddenly?"

"Not anger," Ben said. "So much as fear. I would say that she seemed thoroughly frightened."

85

SEVEN

I couldn't sleep that night. It might have had something to do with the rich food I had consumed at dinner, or the bottle of wine Ben and I had shared — for, needless to say, although the restaurant had appeared to be full, the proprietor had somehow managed to make a small table for two available once Ben had made his presence known. But mainly it was my restless brain and churning thoughts that were to blame for my sleeplessness.

On top of everything else I felt guilty. I had said that I would phone Lynn to tell her of my whereabouts and to let her know if I had been able to make any progress, but in Ben's company the matter had slipped my mind until too late. Now it would have to wait until the following evening, after she returned home from the office.

I stared into the darkness, reaching out for the hundredth time to haul the slippery eiderdown back on to the bed. It was cold — so cold! Where was Simon? Sleeping rough, somewhere on the cliff, or was he somewhere further afield? Maybe I ought to start looking in St Petra, the next-door village along the coast.

Whatever I did that day, it would be without Ben. He had told me the night before that he had agreed months ago to open a charity fête in Plymouth and that he would be leaving around ten o'clock to make sure of getting there by lunchtime. He wasn't looking forward to it, he told me. He had outgrown the adulation, the signing of autographs, all the trappings of fame, and if the charity hadn't been one that was particularly close to his heart he would never have agreed to making an appearance.

I wondered. Was it a pose? No, surely not, for he had voluntarily turned his back on stardom and come to live in Poldrissick, which if not the back-end of nowhere, was not far distant from it. Yet he traded on his celebrity status. That much had been made clear to me several times during the short time I had known him.

And what, I asked myself, could be more human than that? It was a very small thing, really, in return for all the warmth and genuine interest that he dispensed to others.

Had Jessica really been frightened, as he had suggested? Her voice had taken on a shrill edge. I remembered the restless fingers fidgeting with her hair as she had incredulously refuted any chance of Simon sheltering in the Folly. It had sounded like anger to me, but perhaps Ben had been right. Could it have been the possibility of an unknown intruder on her property that had frightened her?

My thoughts circled round and round. Had Max already got to Simon — and what *about* Max? I was prepared to believe all manner of things about him, but stopped short of thinking that he could be a murderer. Ben had gone too far there, I thought. Oh, *damn* this eiderdown! I would never sleep again, I was sure of it.

The next thing I knew, it was seven o'clock and the seagull chorus had started. I groaned as I looked at my watch through a haze of sleep. A church clock chimed. A lorry was revving up in the square. I could hear voices and the clumping of boots on cobblestones. Poldrissick had obviously been awake for some time and there was no hope that I could return to blissful unconsciousness.

I had been dreaming of Jessica, I realised. It had been a jumble of nonsense, as most dreams are, but I knew for certain that we had been together and that we had been friends.

Maybe I explained myself wrongly, I thought. Perhaps if I went to see her again, tried to make her understand that we were merely asking for her help and suggestions, not in any way blaming her for anything, her attitude might be different?

I had nothing to lose, I thought. There was a chance that she herself might feel differently having slept on the matter, particularly if Ben had managed to persuade her that I was no journalist. I resolved that I would go up to the Manor again that very morning.

I got up and dressed, going down to the kitchen to find that Mrs Watkin had provided me with egg and bacon and sausage and tomato, which I ate with pretended enjoyment and no appetite at all. I should be dieting for the next six months, I thought gloomily, if my calorie intake went on at this rate.

Mrs Watkin was in talkative mood, leaning companionably against the sink, watching me consume this gargantuan breakfast as if to make sure that I finished every morsel.

"Did you 'ave a good time with Mr Farrell last night?" she asked. "'E's some lovely en't un? Some 'andsome! Talk to anyone, Mr Farrell would, not like some. Why didn't 'ee tell us you knew un?"

I almost told her of the recent nature of my acquaintance with Ben, but thought better of it. I needed all the help and influence possible — and besides, in Jack Watkin's words, least said, soonest mended. It was no business of hers. Maybe some of the Cornish caution was rubbing off on me.

"Always ready for a laugh, Mr Farrell is," she went

on, a reminiscent light in her eye. "Cor, we've 'ad some times 'ere, I'll tell 'ee! People started off thinking 'Someone famous like that, it won't do to talk to un' but before us knew it, 'e was one o' we."

I must remember to tell him that, I thought. I had the feeling that all the plaudits of the theatre critics would pale into insignificance beside the inhabitants of Poldrissick pronouncing him 'one o' we'.

"Some lovely 'e was in that telly series about the village schoolmaster. I never missed one o' they, not one. Laugh! They all 'eard me one night right through the kitchen wall and into the bar, and next thing I knew I had 'alf a dozen men in 'ere, gogglin' away, just like I was. Seems a shame, like, to 'ave given it all up."

"He's making a great success of writing," I said, realising with a certain wry amusement that I was lapping up Mrs Watkin's praise of him and doing nothing to introduce any other topic of conversation. The pleasure I felt in simply talking about him revealed to me a little more about my feelings for Ben than I was prepared to take.

"'Tain't the same, though, say what you will. I mean, books are all very well . . ." her voice trailed away, leaving me in no doubt at all that they came a very poor second to television. "'Tis nice for 'ee, 'aving a friend 'ere," she went on, obviously feeling that the subject of Ben had not yet been milked dry. "'Tis company, like, while you look for your brother. Are you any nearer finding 'im?"

I shook my head as uttering a long and bloated sigh, I put my knife and fork together neatly on my empty plate.

"Not really. At least I know someone else has been looking for him, which is interesting."

"'Ere —" Mrs Watkin stepped forward from the sink

to remove my plate, but stood still as a thought struck her. "I saw un yesterday, the chap in the blue car. I didn't know till Jack told me that 'e was looking for your brother, too, but I well remember seein' Fred Penhaligon writing out the parking ticket. Well, 'twas fair enough! Right across Beswarick's shopfront, he was — with 'ardly a scrap of room for the delivery van to get by. Some mad, the feller was. 'E come up while Fred was finishing writing and fairly tore the paper out of 'is 'and."

"Where did you see him?" I asked, the moment I could insert a word.

"In St Petra. 'Tis only a l'il tiny place, but there's this great hotel down by the beach where my sister works."

"And that's where you saw him? That's where he's staying?"

"'Im and another chap. The place isn't open properly yet, only a few rooms, so these two had the place to themselves. I reckernised the car the moment I walked up to the hotel."

So now I knew where Max was staying. I sipped my tea thoughtfully, uninterrupted by Mrs Watkin as she had embarked on the washing-up with a great deal of plate-clattering energy.

The telephone rang from the hall outside the kitchen and she pulled a face of resignation as she withdrew her soapy hands from the sink.

"'Tis always the way," she said philosophically. "Ring, ring, ring, that phone never stops."

Her footsteps retreated down the passage, and hardly had she left me when there was a knock on the back door and in came Laurie Barron.

"Well, hallo," he said. "Still having breakfast? It's all right for some — I've been up hours! Where's Emily?"

90

"Mrs Watkin? She's just gone to answer the phone."

"'Tis for you, Miss Kendall," she called out, returning at that moment. Her face changed as she saw Laurie. "What are you doing 'ere?" she asked waspishly. "I thought I told you —"

I did not wait to here what she had told Laurie. I was sure that it must be Ben on the line for me, wanting a quick word before he began his journey to Plymouth.

"Hallo?" I was aware that my pulse rate had increased considerably.

"Sarah?" The voice was masculine, but it did not belong to Ben.

"Yes? Who is that?"

"Don't you know? Three guesses."

I did not need three, or even two.

"Hallo, Max," I said. "I wondered how long it would take you to find me."

"Quite obviously we're down here on the same errand," he said. "We ought to get together. We might be able to help each other."

"What's your angle, Max?" I asked acidly. "It's too much for me to believe that you're motivated by sheer good nature."

"Oh, Sarah, Sarah!" His voice was sorrowful, as if he could hardly believe that anyone could so misjudge him. "Simon went sailing with friends of mine, remember? I've been carrying the most awful feeling of guilt and responsibility ever since the tragedy, so naturally I'm interested in finding out if he's alive or dead. Give me credit for some finer feelings."

I took a deep, slow breath.

"To be honest, Max, I find it hard to give you credit for very much, except for making Lynn desperately unhappy."

"I don't want to talk about Lynn over the telephone. Believe me, she — she —" his voice faltered, and then gathered strength enough to continue. "She's still very important to me, Sarah. Surely we can meet and have a talk? I know you blame me for everything that went wrong, but I can't see why that should prevent us getting together over something as important as finding Simon."

I made no reply as I thought over his words. Nothing he could say would make me trust him, but I felt I could hardly afford not to follow any leads that might be offered me.

"I don't think I can make any suggestions that would be of help," I said. "I've only had a day down here and on the whole people are very close-mouthed. How did you know that Simon might be here?"

"A friend saw him on the television news."

"One of the friends he went sailing with?"

"Yes, as a matter of fact. Does it matter?"

"I merely wondered if you were still in touch with them."

"I happened to run into them at the Sailing Club, that's all. I'm there most weekends, now that — now that there's nothing at home for me any more."

"Pray spare me, you're breaking my heart," I murmured sarcastically.

"Look, Sarah — we can't talk like this. Let's meet, very soon."

"All right," I said, making up my mind suddenly. "Where and when?"

"You name the place and the time."

"All right. I'll see you at your hotel at two o'clock."

I hung up without waiting for his agreement, taking a childish delight in demonstrating that he was not the only one with contacts, that I knew where to find him just as he had known where to find me.

I was not for one moment taken in by the sob-stuff

he had given me, or his claim to finer feelings. The main thing that had interested me was the admission that he was still in touch with the two men. And he had lied about spending every weekend at the Sailing Club. According to the Secretary, he hadn't been near the place for some time — which meant that any meeting had taken place somewhere else.

Suddenly I could hear Ben's voice:

" 'Everything hinges on whether there was any unlawful connection between Max and the two men — if he was only a casual acquaintance, then my theory falls to the ground.' "

It didn't sound as if the three of them were casual acquaintances. Which meant that Ben's theory was a distinct possibility. Which meant that Simon could have found out something discreditable about the two men which also involved Max. Why else, I asked myself, my hand still on the telephone receiver, would Max be so interested in finding Simon?"

Slowly I walked back to the kitchen, intending to thank Mrs Watkin for my nice breakfast, but as I reached the door I could hear her voice raised in anger.

"'Tis the last time I'm telling 'ee," I heard her say.

"Your old man's as glad of it as anyone else, so don't go telling me what to do and what not to do!" Laurie Barron's normally lazy drawl had changed to a tone expressive of intense exasperation. "Bloody women should keep their noses out of it —"

I gave up the notion of going into the kitchen, went upstairs to get my coat, and escaped into the square, but the words stayed with me as I walked round to the car park. Women should keep their noses out of what? Mentally I shook myself. Surely to goodness I had enough to think about without making mysteries out of nothing. He was probably talking about the

Social Club or the Male Voice Choir or the chapel annual outing.

I was not looking forward to seeing Jessica again. I had no confidence at all that she would greet me with any sort of friendliness, however conciliatory my approach, but as I could think of nothing else remotely constructive to do I drove off towards the Manor.

The clouds of yesterday had cleared and it was a perfect spring morning, the sunshine almost warm. It glinted on wet leaves and turned spiders' webs into diamond-spangled ornaments. There were daffodils under the trees along the drive, and pink and white camellias brightening the dark foliage of bushes set deeper in the shrubbery. Birds were singing and lambs bleating from a field that was hidden from me.

As I drove slowly along the winding drive I caught glimpses of the sea, blue as the Mediterranean. So close, I thought. At night one did not realise how close. But then I remembered my sight of the Manor from the small, enclosed beach where the Folly had perched insecurely on the cliff and told myself that the sea's nearness should come as no surprise to me.

Jessica came to the door at once when I rang. She was again dressed in slacks, and I marvelled at the way she made a sweater and smock, of the same kind favoured by Laurie Barron, look like the latest Paris fashion. I smiled at her a little tentatively.

"Forgive me for bothering you again," I said. "I just had to come. I think I must have been clumsy last night, because I had no intention of upsetting you — yet somehow I managed to do so, and I really am sorry."

"My dear, I wasn't in the *least* upset! How nice of you to call." Jessica's smile was apparently genuine.

"Ben told me that you think I'm a journalist, but

I'm not — really, I'm not! I had no idea he lived in Poldrissick. I know the story about my brother Simon sounds crazy, but it's true, every word of it."

"My dear girl, I believe you. Come in and have some coffee and tell me the whole story all over again, and this time I'll listen *frightfully* carefully and will try to be helpful."

The change in her attitude was so total that I was taken aback. I blinked, feeling thoroughly bemused, but followed her inside, perching on a stool in the kitchen while she made coffee, feeling for the moment quite glad that I was called upon to do nothing but listen to her non-stop flow of chatter.

"I know I'm over-protective of Ben," she said, sitting down beside me. "But he's such a poppet, isn't he? I didn't mean to *bristle* at you the way I did. Now go on — tell me everything about your brother all over again."

I began at the beginning.

"It was the day the little boy was found here. You remember the incident, I expect."

"As it happened, I was away from Poldrissick, but of course I heard about it when I got back."

"During the interview, I saw Simon — my brother whom we all thought was dead — walk along the quay towards the village. He was only in view for a second, but neither my sister nor I have any doubts about it. It was Simon, quite definitely. And as Ben pointed out to me, he must either have come from a boat or from the beach."

She was quiet now, listening to me attentively with her cornflower blue eyes open wide and her chin resting on her hand. I still found her calm acceptance of my presence and story hard to reconcile with her agitated manner of the previous evening.

"So you think he could have been living in the

Folly?"

"Only because there's no other cottage or shelter of any kind along that part of the coast. And Cap'n Pengelly said no boat tied up that Sunday."

"Then we'd better go and look at it," she said. "Just to satisfy you that there's no one there."

We went outside together. Nothing could have been more friendly than the way she took my arm to draw me in the right direction, no one more animated and full of charm. I began to wonder if I had dreamed the hostility she had shown before.

"We go down this little path behind the trees and across the meadow," she said. "Watch where you're treading. Mr Pollard keeps his cows here sometimes. Well, not cows actually but steers — still, the result is the same as far as the meadow is concerned . . ."

A voice hailed us loudly from the direction of the house, and Jessica turned. A small, wizened man in a black anorak and a woolly hat was waving an axe and shouting something incomprehensible.

"Oh dear," Jessica said. "That's Eddie, one of the gardeners. Really, it's so difficult conversing with the dear creature — one can't understand a word he says, his accent is so broad. He's a maniac about cutting down trees and I'm always having to restrain him. I'd better go and have a soothing word before the whole estate resounds to cries of 'Timber!' You go on if you like. Here, take the key. Just follow this path to the cliff and you'll see the way easily enough."

The meadow ended in a wire fence at the top of the cliff, but there was a gate which showed the way to a tiny, overgrown path from where I could look down on the building known as the Folly. My first impression was that it was very small and my second that the roof was in good repair, considering that it had apparently not been in use for a generation.

96

It perched on a ledge roughly a third of the way down the cliff. The reason I had not been able to see the path to it from the beach below was because it was hardly discernible, even from above, the gorse bushes grew so thickly on either side. I could smell the heady, coconut scent of the yellow flowers, warmed by the sun, as I picked my way downwards. The path descended steeply and I needed all my concentration to negotiate it safely, so that when I finally arrived at the level portion of the cliff on which the tiny house stood, the strangeness of it at close quarters took me unawares.

It was built in a wedge shape, the pointed end set in a crevice of the cliff, the wide end facing the sea. The door, which was in the side wall, was of solid wood with large, decorative iron hinges as if the builder had tried to make it match the Manor to which it belonged, but although the slate roof seemed sound, as I had noted from above, the stonework masonry was crumbling and in one place a sheet of corrugated iron had been roughly battened over a hole in the wall.

The key moved easily enough and I went inside. The room was, perhaps, ten feet at its widest part, narrowing down to little more than three or four, and from end to end it was no longer than twelve feet — perhaps less. Tall sash windows, three in number, spanned the wide end looking on to the sea, and I walked straight over to them to look out on the turbulent waves below me which now pounded on the rocks which circled the small cove. I felt like an eagle in its eyrie, I was so far above them.

Beyond the darker waters of the inlet, the sea was blue and it sparkled in the sun, looking beautiful and benign. Here, as I looked down, I thought it was no less beautiful — but this was a different, terrible sort of beauty, wild and untamed, the crashing waves deep green and unfathomable. It was hard to believe that this was the sandy little beach where, at low tide, I had stood the day before. And where someone else had stood, watching me.

I turned from the windows and looked at the rest of the small room. The walls had once been plastered and painted, but they were now in a bad state of repair, scabrous with damp rot. There was no furniture and, as Ben had said, no services — no water or light. If Simon had indeed slept here, it would have been a spartan existence — which meant little, for creature comforts had never meant much to him. He and his friends had hitch-hiked and camped their way around most of Europe before now and might often have been glad of shelter even as poor as this.

In the narrow corner of the room I looked curiously at three solid pieces of wood, roughly three feet across and perhaps ten feet high, which leaned against the wall. Jessica joined me as I was studying them.

"You see — absolutely nothing and nobody here," she said.

"No. Well, it was always a long shot, I suppose. I'm interested to have seen it, anyway. Who built it in the first place?"

"The Trewartha before the Trewartha before last. He'd served in India, in some remote place on the frontier, and like Garbo, he wanted to be alone. He was supposed to be writing a treatise on seabirds, so the story goes, but it's my belief he simply wanted to withdraw from family life." She looked around the place and smiled. "Since then it's been used for romantic assignations, youthful indulgence in forbidden cigarettes and alcohol, and once even for attempted murder. Oh, yes — it's said that George's grandfather caught his wife and a common fisherman *in flagrante delicto* and attempted to shoot him with

98

an airgun. Fortunately, he wasn't a very good shot."

"So he lived to fish again! I wonder if he was an ancestor of Laurie Barron?"

Jessica laughed.

"More than likely. Everyone's related to everyone else in Poldrissick. If you're not a Barron, you're a Beswarick or a Nancarrow — or possibly a mixture of all three."

"What are these things for?" I asked, looking again at the wooden battens that leaned against the wall.

"Typhoon shutters."

"What?" I looked at her with a puzzled frown, half laughing. It sounded like yet another of her exaggerated expressions.

"No, really. Everyone had them in Hong Kong, for obvious reasons. We never knew when we might need them. And the same is true here. Oh, no one calls them typhoons, of course, but I can assure you that in gale force winds, when the black cone is hoisted at the coastguard station, the rain pours in here and does an enormous amount of damage. Those fit over the windows."

"So you are interested in preserving the place! Do you think you'll ever make it habitable?"

"No, not really. Well, I have vague plans for restoring it as a sort of summerhouse, but I don't suppose they'll come to anything. I'm just not ready to write it off yet. Have you seen enough?"

I had. If Simon had ever been there, there was no trace of him now. I thanked her for showing me the place and turned to leave it with a sigh of disappointment.

Jessica followed me up the path silently, and I was too occupied with my own thoughts to realise at the time how unusual this was. We stood for a moment on the cliff, looking at the incomparable view and

99

regaining our breath.

"I hope you're doing the right thing," Jessica said suddenly, in a voice that was sober and quiet, very different from her usual extravagant tones.

"How do you mean?"

"This brother of yours — Simon. It has struck you, I suppose, that he could have good reason for not wanting to be found?"

"Yes, it has. That's why my sister and I decided to make our own inquiries."

She was looking at me very intently and seemed about to speak. I waited for a moment, but either I had been mistaken or she thought better of it. She looked again at the horizon and said nothing.

"Besides," I went on. "We know now that someone else is looking for him, so any secrecy is pointless —"

"Who's looking for him?" She turned to me sharply. "Who else is interested?"

I hesitated. It was such a long and involved story, so unbelievable by anybody's standards. Previously we had merely mentioned that Simon had been believed dead, but that I had happened to see him on television and had come to Poldrissick to look for him.

"Do you mean the police?" she went on, as I said nothing.

"No, no. My sister's ex-husband."

"I see."

Abruptly she turned to lead the way back to the house and I fell into step beside her, prepared to elaborate. She knew so much, I felt, I might just as well give her more details, since it seemed I had captured her interest at last. It was just possible that she could help.

She gave me no chance. With a return to her former garrulity she began talking of all she had done to the Manor and its grounds, pointing out a rhododendron

100

bush of a particularly rare species that was about to burst into flower, leading me through a plantation of azaleas.

"In another couple of weeks this will really be something to see," she said. "All those rhododendrons literally blaze with colour, cascading down from an enormous height. And the azaleas — I love them particularly. They grow wild in Hong Kong, you know."

"They must be beautiful."

"Oh, they are, they are." She seemed to be aware that I had spoken absently, and put her arm through mine. "Don't look so worried," she went on. "I'm quite sure your brother can look after himself."

"He's resourceful enough," I admitted. "It's the whys and wherefores that puzzle me. If only he'd made some sort of contact! It isn't like him to be so thoughtless. He'd know exactly how my sister and I would feel when we heard about the accident."

"Perhaps you ought to trust him more," she said. "I still think he might have his own reasons for keeping quiet." As before, I had the impression that she was making up her mind to say more and I looked at her questioningly. We had stopped by an iron kissing-gate that led to the more formal lawns and rose gardens in front of the Manor and for a second she stood by it, swinging it idly as if lost in thought. But she said nothing, merely holding the gate open for me to precede her. For a few yards we walked in single file towards the house.

"Are you in love with Ben?" she asked me suddenly. I stopped and looked round at her.

"Good Lord, no," I said, with a laugh. "I hardly know him. We only met yesterday."

"My dear girl, what on earth does that have to do with it? We women fall in love largely through our imaginations and I'm the first to admit that there's

101

something about Ben that captures the imagination of most women, from fourteen to forty, and far beyond. He can be the most entertaining of companions. He's lively and amusing and has that very special quality of making a woman feel that whatever she says is the most fascinating thing he's ever heard — but oh, my dear, I've seen that look so often, cast in so many different directions."

"I know his name's been linked with a number of actresses."

"All very beautiful and talented and glamorous."

While I, I thought grimly, had — to quote Ben — a very nice little face. What was that quotation about damning with faint praise?

Jessica squeezed my arm.

"I hope you don't mind my talking to you like this. I would simply hate you to read too much into his interest. It's the way he is."

"Don't worry. I never for one moment imagined that I should see him again once I'd left Poldrissick."

"Sensible girl!"

She smiled, a smile that ended on a sigh. Absently she picked a daffodil and twisted it in her hand.

"Life's not always easy, is it?" she said obscurely, not smiling any more. "And love's the very devil."

So *that* was it! In spite of the difference in their years, she was in love with Ben and was warning me away from her property. I felt that I understood everything now, from the hostility of the previous evening, to her question about my relationship with him.

Her face was strained, the lines around her mouth more obvious.

"And age is the very devil," she said tightly. Her step quickened and the flower she held in her hand drooped and was crushed.

"But you're still lovely," I blurted out, feeling some embarrassment in the light of all that Ben had said to me about her.

"Ah!" She turned and gave me a small, thin smile. "The sting is in the word 'still'. It implies a somewhat precarious position — a state that isn't going to continue for very long."

I murmured something inarticulate, not knowing how to reply to this. To say 'You've had a good innings' would be harsh and unsympathetic, but it was the phrase that immediately occurred to me.

Her expression lightened and playfully she tapped me with the broken flower.

"Never mind the maunderings of an ageing socialite! I have a few good years left in me yet and I mean to make the most of them." She sighed theatrically. "If only one could find men of one's own age even *remotely* attractive! One's so conscious of balding heads and pot bellies and false teeth."

I laughed at her. Clearly she was back in form again, exaggerating wildly and extracting amusement in doing so.

I declined her offer of coffee, thanked her for letting me look at the Folly, and drove back to the village. I felt vaguely depressed, but did not know whether this was because of Jessica's warning about Ben or because the Folly had yielded no clue to Simon's whereabouts. Perhaps it was a mixture of both, which, I told myself, was nothing short of foolish, since my expectations in neither direction had been high. I had recognised all along that my association with Ben was transitory; and as for the Folly, I had been grasping at straws, nothing more. What could it have told me?

I was washing my hands in my room at the Anchor, thinking to myself that the decor was unimportant

103

compared to the fact that the place was spotlessly clean, when suddenly it hit me like one of Jessica's typhoons. If no one ·had visited the Folly for ages, as she had stated, why was it so clean? Oh, it was in disrepair, that was true —plaster had fallen from the wall and the whole building seemed to sag. Yet there was no plaster on the floor. The strong winds had not blown dirt or leaves under the door. It looked freshly swept and smelled clean and sweet as if it had been aired frequently.

I felt annoyed with myself that I had not commented on this to Jessica at the time. Perhaps she herself made a point of seeing that it was swept occasionally, yet somehow it seemed unlikely. She had recently been away from Poldrissick, she had been fully occupied with the flat in the west wing, and as far as I could gather, she ran the garden with the minimum of help.

It didn't mean anything, of course, but it struck me as odd. It hardly proved that Simon had been there, but equally it didn't prove that he hadn't. An accumulation of dirt would have convinced me once and for all that he had not made the Folly his hiding-place, for although he was untidy and thought nothing of wearing tattered jeans that would disgrace any self-respecting hobo, he was fanatical about cleanliness.

But what about the fact that there was no light or water or sanitation?

I sank down on the edge of the bed and stared into space, trying to imagine how he would have coped. It was hard to do so — but then I had never been the outdoor type. I had been a half-hearted Girl Guide, developing into an unenthusiastic camper, whereas Simon had frequently disappeared into the wilds for weeks on end, had proved his resourcefulness on numerous occasions.

It was impossible, though, not to come up against the main objection to this theory. If he had at any time stayed in the Folly, then Jessica would surely have known of it.

He could not approach it other than through her land. If she walked along the cliff as often as she claimed, she surely would have seen some sign of him.

Perhaps she had, I thought. Perhaps for reasons best known to herself, she had been secretly sheltering Simon. That would account for her reaction when I questioned her and would certainly explain how Simon had been able to survive there, for with her co-operation many of the practical difficulties would melt away.

She could have rushed down there after we left the Manor the previous night, warned Simon that I was hot on his trail, and moved him out, lock, stock and barrel, so that this morning she could, with a clear conscience, invite me to take a look around the place myself, sure that I would find nothing there. Except those so-called typhoon shutters, which were heavy and would have been difficult to drag up the steep path.

I sat up straighter. She had expleained their existence by saying that they kept out the wind and the rain, but given that someone was secretly sheltering there, they could have another purpose too. They would effectively keep out any light at night, for otherwise passing fishing-boats would soon know that the place was occupied. It was possible. It was definitely possible.

I sighed and sagged with depression again. Why? That was the question that was impossible to answer. Why would Simon entrust himself to Jessica and hide from me? That was something I could not explain, however much I thought around the subject.

I longed to be able to talk to Ben. Damn it, I thought – there's another thing! You know Jessica is right. You know he will have forgotten you five minutes after you've left Poldrissick. No girl with any sense at all would allow herself to fall in love with him.

I was beginning to think that I hadn't got the sense I was born with.

EIGHT

St Petra was quite a different kind of village from Poldrissick. Here there were no cliffs and no harbour, and the few shops and houses were strung out along a sandy beach where, at the far end, the Rock Hotel dominated the skyline.

On this bright, sunny April Saturday, a number of people were enjoying the air and the hotel car-park was almost full. Two youths were standing close to the metallic blue Porsche and looking at it covetously.

Max was sitting in the hotel lounge at a table in the bay window that overlooked the beach and a wide expanse of sea. He hadn't changed a bit. He still looked sleek and handsome and pleased with himself, and he rose to greet me as if we were good friends, kissing my cheek so that I caught a whiff of the expensive after-shave lotion I always associated with him.

"Lovely to see you," he said. "You look marvellous."

"And you look — just as usual."

With a great effort I managed to keep my voice friendly, feeling that only by doing so was I likely to learn anything from him. And it needed an effort, for I had never liked him and it was too late to begin now. Even if I had entertained any doubts about Lynn's wisdom in divorcing him — which I never had — his petty vindictiveness since had made me quite certain that she had done the right thing.

"Would you like some coffee?"

"Please don't bother."

"Cigarette? You don't mind if I do?"

I waited for him to light the cigarette and put the gold lighter back in his pocket before I spoke.

"Max, why are you down here looking for Simon? I find all that business about your feelings of guilt and responsibility awfully hard to swallow."

He smiled and shrugged.

"You always have put the worst possible interpretation on my actions. Tell me, how's Lynn?"

"Very well."

"I'm thankful to hear it. I can't tell you how I long to see her, in spite of the way she treated me."

I didn't know whether to be amused or angry at this. Lynn was, like the rest of us, by no means faultless, but she had remained loyal to Max long after most wives would have left him. He had continually belittled her, sapped her self-confidence, lied to her and betrayed her, and through it all she had behaved with great dignity and had never complained even to me until everything had become past bearing. And when finally she could take no more she had left without making undue financial demands.

"I don't think we'd better begin discussing that question," I said, with what I considered great self-restraint.

"As you please. Nevertheless, it's part of the reason that I'm here. I want to find Simon for Lynn's sake. The moment I heard he'd been seen, my first reaction was to phone her and tell her the good news, but on reflection I didn't dare to, just in case the whole thing was a mistake."

"So you dropped all your important business interests to come and find him?"

"That's exactly right." He tapped the ash off his cigarette with a quick, nervous movement, his eyes not meeting mine. "I thought that perhaps if I could find him, it might go a long way to healing the breach between Lynn and me." He spoke in a clipped voice as if doing his best to control his emotion.

"Heal the breach?" I echoed incredulously.

"Sarah, nothing has been the same since she left me. I can't get enthusiastic about my job any more. I drink too much. Life holds nothing for me."

If I didn't know him so well, I thought, I could almost be taken in. He was giving a wonderful performance of a man in the grip of suffering almost beyond endurance. I felt like giving him a round of applause.

"Oh, what a pity," I said, in brightly conversational tones. "Have you ever thought of ending it all?"

"My God, Sarah, you're hard!"

"Well, really! You can't honestly expect me to take all that rubbish seriously, can you? We both know how it was with you and Lynn. Besides, trying to convince me how wronged you are is quite pointless — in the last analysis it's what she thinks that counts. The only reason I agreed to meet you was to talk about Simon. What have you managed to find out?"

He looked annoyed and petulant and for a moment said nothing, stubbing out his cigarette in the ashtray.

"Not a lot," he said at last. "In my view, he must be suffering from loss of memory. He could have suffered a blow on the head which caused a blackout. He might have no idea of his real name or circumstances."

"For someone as confused as that, he's doing a pretty good job of hiding himself. Do you have a theory about how he got from Cannes to Poldrissick."

"That's comparatively simple. He could have hitched a lift easily enough. There are plenty of yachts sailing between Cornwall and France during the summer. Someone could have found him wandering

— someone who was about to come home, and who simply gave him a ride back to England rather than get involved with all the gendarmerie over there."

"So where is he now? Haven't you been able to find out anything?"

"I'm almost certain he's gone from the district. No one has seen him since last Sunday — almost a week ago."

"Perhaps he's regained his memory at last and gone home," I said. It was an idle suggestion. I did not believe in the loss of memory theory and I knew for certain that Simon was still missing when I left London three days previously, but Max took me up on it immediately.

"It wouldn't surprise me if you're right. Look — you go home so that you're there if he should turn up at your flat. It would be frightful for him to go there only to find it empty —"

I had a sudden mental picture of Simon as I had seen him on that last occasion, sitting on my doorstep. The thought of him sitting there again, waiting and waiting for me to come home, the night growing colder, filled me with a momentary panic. Just for a second Max had almost convinced me that my best plan was to go home so that I was on the spot if needed.

"I'll stay down for a few more days," he went on. "I'll keep in touch by phone —"

"I don't think so, Max."

"Please yourself!" He looked irritated that I had not immediately fallen in with his suggestion. Once more he took out his cigarette case.

"Are you sure you won't have one? No? I smoke too much, I admit it. I smoke even more, since Lynn ... but it's no use talking to you about that, of course." He blew smoke in my direction lazily. "Still, cigarettes aren't the only things that can damage your health, you know."

"Of course not."

"Take that placid-looking sea out there." He nodded towards the window. "It's so deep, so vast. Strictly between you and me, even though I've sailed for most of my life, I'm terrified of it. Perhaps *because* I've sailed for most of my life. One begins to respect the power of the elements, when one's miles out of sight of land. Many a time I've felt a shiver down my spine, even on the calmest day, when I've thought of the depth of the water under the keel." He turned and looked at me, smiling slightly. "Anyone could disappear without trace," he went on. "Anyone. Even the most experienced sailor."

He had succeeded in making me very frightened.

"You surprise me," I said, hoping that my voice showed no trace of my sudden fear. "I imagined you to be quite intrepid."

He laughed softly.

"That just shows how wrong you can be. I'm scared to death of a number of things."

"Like domesticity?" I asked sweetly.

"You don't give up, do you? Actually at that precise moment I was thinking of poverty."

"Poverty!" I laughed. "That's something you've never had to worry about. You were born with the proverbial silver spoon in your mouth."

He looked at me with a strange smile, his eyebrows lifted, and said nothing.

"Well," I began, picking up my handbag and my coat. "We don't seem to have helped each other very much, do we? I think you're wasting your time here, Max. You ought to get back to your business —"

"Hey, Max!" Someone was crossing the room towards him, calling out to him, and I was conscious of

Max frowning with annoyance. The stranger was a thin, sharp-featured young man wearing jeans and a leather jacket of the type worn by motorcyclists.

"What is it?" Max asked tersely, obviously embarrassed that others in the room were turning to see who was being hailed so loudly.

"It's Cloutier on the phone for you. You'd better jump."

Without a word, Max jumped. He rose from his chair and strode towards the door, leaving the black-coated young man staring down at me with a grin on his face.

"Hi," he said. "My name's Paul. You're Simon Kendall's sister, aren't you?"

"Yes — do you know him?"

He laughed.

"Know him? I went sailing with him, didn't I?"

He had a whiny voice with a London accent, and he chewed gum as he spoke to me.

"*You* went sailing with him!"

"That's right. One of the original three, I was."

"And you came to help Max look for him. How kind."

"Well, Simon was me mate, wasn't he?"

"Was he?" I frowned at him in disbelief. "I thought you quarrelled. He told me the boat was too small for the three, of you."

He chewed for a moment in silence.

"What else did he tell you?" he asked.

"Only that he was leaving you and joining up with some others."

"Because they were going on to Cannes, that's why. There wasn't no quarrel — not more than a few words, like you get any time when you're banged up with the same people day after day. Me and Ted — the other chap who was with us — we had to come

112

back, but Simon wanted to go on. That's all it was. I'd sail with Simon again any time." He pointed a finger at me to emphasise his words. "In fact I'll take a bet with you. Simon will be on my boat again in a matter of days."

"Really?" I had not taken to this erstwhile companion of Simon's and in fact found it hard to believe that Simon could have gone sailing with him in the first place. And how did such a little pipsqueak come to own a boat, anyway? I began walking to the door and Paul fell in beside me.

"Just bought a new one," he said. "A real beauty. Only collected it this morning. It's a Helford Cutter, sloop rigged – a real quality job. Straight up – it's moored at Lamladroc."

"It sounds wonderful," I said, only half listening. Something else was tugging at my consciousness.

"Yeah. Simon won't be able to resist it." He laughed as if he had made a joke, and I smiled absently, suddenly remembering what had been worrying me.

"This Mr Cloutier who has just phoned Max —"

"Monsieur Cloutier," Paul corrected me. "Monsieur from Paris, where the crumpet comes from."

I bent to fit the key into the door of my car.

"How is Pierre?" I asked. "It's such a long time since I've seen him."

Paul made no reply and when I looked up at him he was frowning at me, chewing in a reflective sort of a way.

"I didn't know you knew him," he said.

"Of course I know him! You forget I was once related to Max. I know a great number of his friends."

"Not so much a *friend* . . ." Paul was mumbling now, awkwardly aware that he might have said too much. He shifted his weight from one foot to the other. "Yeah, well, I'd better be off, I expect."

113

I wouldn't let him go as easily as that.

"Does Max still do a lot of business with Pierre?" I asked.

His eyes shifted away, uneasy and vaguely anxious.

"I wouldn't know," he said. "It's nothing to do with me."

"No, of course not. Nor me." I smiled at him as I started the engine. "I was merely making polite conversation. Say goodbye to Max for me."

I gave him a small wave and drove out of the car park.

Idiot boy, I thought as I drove. He's told me all I want to know. If Pierre Cloutier was phoning from Paris about parts for cars, then why had Paul grown so shifty and evasive, all of a sudden? Why suddenly had he known nothing about Cloutier, when previously he'd said to Max 'You'd better jump', implying that they both knew Cloutier called the shots? Why on earth was the elegant, Saville-Row-suited Max associating with someone like Paul in the first place? Quite apart from the difference in their social backgrounds, Max must have been anything from ten to fifteen years older than Paul, whom I judged to be around twenty-three or four.

And how, I asked myself again, had such a young man accumulated enough money to buy a yacht worth thousands? He could have won the pools, of course, though somehow I didn't think so. One thing was sure. He hadn't earned it by the use of his brains. I smiled grimly to myself as I wondered what Max would have said, had he heard Paul's poor attempt at evasion just now.

And then I stopped smiling. Ben had been right. The whole thing was far bigger than we had thought. Max had been tied up with the two men, and not only Max but Pierre Cloutier, too, who, according to

Lynn's testimony, was a nasty piece of work who was unlikely to object to some lucrative smuggling.

For this, I was now sure, was what it was all about. Ben had been right about that, too. Which meant that I *had* to find Simon to warn him that Max and his friends were looking for him.

It was all falling into place. Max had tried to dissuade Simon from joining the other two because he must have known that Paul, if not the unknown Ted, was certainly not bright enough to keep the true reason for the journey from Simon. And he would know that Simon would have strong objections to what they were doing.

And Simon did find out, and he did object, and he left the others — perhaps threatening to go to the police. Or even if he hadn't threatened, they would still regard him as a potential hazard to them, since he knew too much about them.

So an accident had been arranged and two innocent men had died — but Simon, for whom the whole thing had been staged, had somehow escaped and had successfully hidden himself until the day he had strayed into the orbit of the television camera.

They had tried to murder him once and they intended to try again. Simon wouldn't be able to resist sailing with him, Paul had said. Anyone could disappear without trace out there, Max had said.

I pulled into the side of the lane and took a map out of the glove compartment. Paul had given a jerk of his chin in the general direction of Poldrissick when he had mentioned the place where he had moored his new boat. What was the name of it? Something strange and unfamiliar and very Cornish.

And then I saw it. Lamladroc. It was nothing more than a tiny indentation in the coastline, nearer to Poldrissick than to St Petra, and it looked as if there was nothing bigger than a footpath on which to approach it. The road was going inland at the point where I had stopped. There should be a right turn after a mile or so which would take me away from the main Poldrissick to St Petra road, back in the direction of the sea, after which I should have to park and walk.

I found the footpath easily enough, clearly marked with a signpost to Lamladroc Cove. Two walkers were emerging from it as I parked the car and they smiled and said that it had been a lovely afternoon but that the warmth had already gone out of the sun.

I saw no one else on the path. The gorse on each side of me was head-high, the vegetation thick and impenetrable. There were hawthorn bushes, twisted into grotesque shapes by the prevailing wind, and dense thickets of sloes and elders and stunted oaks.

For a long while I could not see the sea, for the path seemed to plunge downwards, so shaded by the trees and bushes that the sun had not penetrated to it and it was still muddy with deep puddles in the hollows. But then suddenly I was out of this dark and enclosed place and there was nothing but springy grass between me and the cliff. The path followed the line of the coast, a few strands of wire fencing all that protected the walker from the sheer drop on his left hand.

The warmth had indeed gone out of the sun and the blue sky had faded, its brilliance screened by a light haze. There seemed no other living soul in the universe. I felt small and unimportant, dwarfed by the spectacular scenery, the gigantic sweep of sea and sky.

The path curved inland again and emerged after a few dark, bush-shaded yards directly on to the cliff top, and here I was not alone. An old man stood looking down into the small cove which lay revealed beneath us.

He turned and nodded a greeting as he sensed my approach.

"'Afternoon," he said, his neck protruding from his hunched shoulders like a plucked turkey. "Wind's getting up."

"Is this Lamladroc?" I asked him.

"Ah, 'tis that."

"And that boat out there," I said, pointing to the yacht that rocked gently in the centre of the cove. "Would that be a Helford Cutter?"

"Danged if I know what they do call un, my bird, but I'll tell 'ee one thing — better fit the owner paid harbour dues and sailed 'er into Poldrissick. Must be some furriner as put 'er there. No local man would belong to do that."

"Oh? Isn't the cove safe?"

"'Tis safe enough once you'm over the Romillies, but 'tis a tricky passage. They rocks are some fierce, maid, I'm tellin' 'ee. There's no going in or out of Lamladroc save at 'igh tide." He shook his head at the folly of the boat-owner. "Must be a furriner," he said again, as if that would explain all.

I had a momentary vision of a Russian with snow on his boots, but remembered that to a Cornishman, a 'furriner' was anyone living east of the Tamar.

"So whoever it is is stuck there till high tide, is he?" I asked.

"Tha'ss it, my 'andsome." He produced a watch on a chain from an inside pocket. "Which is in 'alf an hour exactly. I wonder where 'ee's to? Let's 'ope the bleddy fool knows about the Romillies. 'Tes nothin' short of criminal, the way anyone can sail a boat round 'ere without the least bit 'o local knowledge."

He shook his head and muttered for a little longer,

said that for his part, he'd let the bleddy fool get on with it and serve 'im right if that 'andsome craft was 'oled.

He eyed the offending boat with an air of lugubrious displeasure and stumped off disapprovingly, into the bushes and out of my sight.

I continued to look at the beautiful boat below me. Sailing had never been a hobby of mine, but I knew enough about it to recognise that anyone buying that vessel wouldn't see much change out of twenty thousand pounds.

How very foolish not to have moored it in the safety of the harbour! What could have possessed the man — unless, of course, as the old fisherman had suggested, he was totally ignorant of local conditions. Or, perhaps, prized secrecy above everything, for there could be few coves more remote from a road than this one. To the north-east the view of the coast was limited, though the sea seemed to stretch to infinity. To the south-west, I realised that as the crow might fly, I was not so very far distant from the Manor and the small, rocky beach that lay beneath the Folly. There was a visible path again following the coastline, disappearing from time to time as it bent and dipped to follow the contours of the land, but always reappearing to continue on so that I felt sure it would be an easy matter to walk back to Poldrissick if I had so desired.

I did not so desire, for the car was waiting for me back at the beginning of the path. I was reluctant to return to it just yet, though. I continued to look at the cutter, biting my lip and frowning with concentration. There must, I thought, be something I could do to stave off the inevitable attempt on Simon's life. I had no doubt whatever that if Max and Paul should find him before I did, the three of them

118

would sail away on that boat — but only two would come back.

I considered sabotage, but rejected it immediately, for although the idea was attractive it was also totally impractical. The cutter was moored thirty yards out in the bay — not, perhaps, a long swim for some, but one which I did not feel competent to undertake in those icy waters. Also, I had no means of carrying out any such sabotage. Added to which, not only would I be putting myself totally in the wrong in the eyes of the law, but I would personally find it all but impossible to harm such a beautiful craft.

There would be a dinghy though, I thought suddenly. Paul would hardly have anchored the cutter and swum ashore. No doubt he would have beached a small boat somewhere under the cliff out of my sight.

A dighy would be a somewhat different matter. I could bring myself to put that out of action, and while it might not prevent an attempt on Simon's life, it might at least buy a little valuable time. And having done that, I thought, I would quite definitely go to the police and tell them everything. Things were too dangerous now to hold back any longer.

I looked for a way down into the cove and found it easily enough. It meant walking round the curve of the bay where the cliff was slightly less steep, scrambling down it for a few feet, and then negotiating some very easily climbable rocks.

It was a perfect little beach, crescent shaped and sandy. I could see the waves breaking on the rocks that the old boy had mentioned, but here in the sheltering arms of the cove, they murmured gently on the sand and placidly lapped the hull of the cutter.

I could see no dinghy, but at first was not dismayed as rocky outcrops provided plenty of hiding-

119

places. A small boat could have been hidden in the shelter of any one of them.

There were a few shallow caves, too, and I looked inside all of them. There was no dinghy.

Oh, well! It had been a good try. I would walk back to the road, I thought, and drive at once to the police station in Falmouth. Somehow I would have to convince somebody to take this thing seriously, even though it sounded like the purest fiction.

I shivered. It was now definitely cold, the sunny afternoon over. I turned away from the last little cave I had been inspecting and stopped dead. Even from that side of the bay I could see that the tide was rushing in over the seaweed-covered rocks where I had made my descent.

It *couldn't* have happened so quickly! For a split second I stood immobile, shocked into disbelief, but then I began to run across to the other side, my feet sinking into the sand at every step. They felt as if ton weights had been fixed to them.

Even when I stood on the rapidly diminishing stretch of sand within feet of the rocks I could hardly believe the evidence of my own eyes. It must be a mistake, I thought wildly. Some freak of nature that had caused the sea to come in too quickly, and just as quickly it would surely disappear so that the rocks would emerge again.

I swore at myself and my own foolishness, and panic-stricken, turned to study the cliffs which seemed to look even steeper now. I'd have to try it, I thought – there was no other way. And at least once I had managed to climb the first rocky stretch, there were bushes and shrubs to hang on to; with shallow roots, I reminded myself. There was no soil there to hold them firmly.

I looked up and shuddered – looked back at the

ever-encroaching tide and shuddered still more. I had no choice at all. I would have to go up.

The first few feet were easier than I had expected. The rocky lower reaches of the cliff had plenty of footholds, and I felt that perhaps I had overestimated the difficulties — until I looked up and saw the cliffs rearing above me. I had never felt so alone. I stopped to regain my breath and forced myself to think calmly, to plan ahead, to search out the best places to put my feet, the best handholds. Somehow I managed to advance a few more feet, and my spirits rose a little.

I reached above my head for a root of a bush that seemed to form a kind of loop and gave a yelp as it came away in my hand. For a few seconds I pressed myself against the cliff, my heart hammering, certain that I would have to stay there, that I could not bring myself to move again. But then I saw a ledge slightly up and to the right of me, and with infinite caution I inched myself towards it and managed to gain a firm foothold.

I thought I heard someone calling, but one glance downward made me close my eyes with renewed panic. I would not do that again, I vowed. I wouldn't look anywhere but a foot above my head.

Again I heard a voice. I clung to a rock and looked cautiously upwards. Sweat was pouring down my forehead and my hair was plastered across my eyes. I could not spare a hand to remove it, but dimly I could see a figure above me and a shower of stones rattled down, hitting me on the head.

"Go away!" I shouted, conscious only that an avalanche could dislodge me altogether. More stones hurtled down the cliff. I moved my head sideways and was rewarded by the sight of a comparatively safe-looking ledge over to my left. Perhaps, I thought, if I managed to reach it I would be safe from the maniac above me.

For the moment I did not ask myself who it could be, I was too occupied with second-to-second survival; but the moment I reached the ledge and felt slightly less insecure physically, panic swept over me. It had to be Paul, coming to take his boat over the rocks because now was the time.

I clung to a bush and strained to look upwards. I could see denim-clad legs descending towards me.

"Go away," I said again — not shouting this time, for my voice emerged in a kind of hoarse, terrified whisper.

The bush half tore away from the cliff. Shuddering, feeling that I had used up all my strength, all my determination, I crouched on the ledge with my eyes closed, my cheek pressed against a slab of granite.

The man above me came nearer. Stones rattled down. My blood seemed to turn to ice-water, for if Paul and Max were to ensure that Simon was to disappear without trace in that vast, heaving sea out there, I could see no reason on earth why my fate would not be precisely the same.

Still nearer he came. There was a final pattering of earth on my hair and the scrape and bump of someone landing on the ledge beside me.

"You *bloody* idiot!" said a familiar voice.

I pushed the hair out of my now open eyes and stared at the owner of it in astonishment.

"Oh, Simon," I said, my voice emerging as a sob. "Oh, Simon!"

"Well, don't for God's sake cry," he said. "Aren't you pleased to see me?"

NINE

I babbled incoherently, but firmly he told me to concentrate on climbing.

"Explanations can come later," he said. "And, by God, they'd better be good."

"What do you *mean*?"

"What the hell you're doing here I can't imagine! I've been watching you for the last half-hour. I couldn't believe you'd be such a twit as to let yourself get caught by the tide — no, dummy, don't put your foot there — go on up a bit, there, to your right. Got it? OK. Now lean on me and reach for that jutting piece of rock. I've got you. Of all the fool things to do! Are you all right there? Well, hang on and I'll go up a bit and give you a hoist. Don't look down, whatever you do."

I was too pleased to see him to take any notice of the abuse, which I knew he didn't mean anyway. It did occur to me to wonder, with a brief flicker of annoyance, why I was the one who owed the explanations, but I was too busy with my inch-by-inch progress up the cliff to give this point my full attention. When finally he reached the clifftop ahead of me and leaned over to give me one last hand up, he paused and grinned, my hand held firmly in his.

"So pleased to make your acquaintance," he said.

Winded, I flopped forward on the wiry grass, totally unable to do more than gasp.

"If you don't mind," he said, after a few moments, "I'd very much prefer to get under cover. I'm not exactly wild about advertising my presence like this. If you can manage to follow me for a bit, I know a rather useful hollow in the gorse.

I rolled over and propped myself on my elbows, still panting.

"You're an absolute bastard, not letting us know you were all right," I managed to gasp.

"I told you I was dropping out of sight. I told you I'd be in touch as soon as I possibly could."

"You didn't tell us anything!"

His expression changed. The annoyance drained from his face and was replaced by a look of horror.

"My God," he said. "You mean you thought I was dead?"

I nodded, still struggling for breath.

He looked at me in shocked silence for a second, then gave a swift look over his shoulder.

"Come on," he said. "Let's get under cover. It's only a few yards – it's a pretty good hideout."

I couldn't help laughing at that, for it held so many echoes from the past. How many times, I wondered, had the two of us retreated to one of Simon's hideouts, escaping from teas with visiting aunts, chores that we should have carried out? I took his hand and allowed myself to be pulled to my feet. He put an arm around my shoulder and gave me a brief squeeze.

"I'm sorry, Sal," he said. "I wouldn't knowingly have put you through that."

I felt better just knowing that, even though nothing made any sense to me. I should have trusted him, I thought, just as Jessica had said. Funny that she should have said that, just as if she had known that he would have tried to get in touch.

We went away from the clifftop path, up a steep field where the gorse grew thickly. He pulled one

124

bush aside and revealed a narrow path which we followed with great difficulty for a few yards until it widened into a grassy clearing, just big enough for the two of us to sit in comfort. Simon had obviously made it his own. There was a rucksack leaning against a small hawthorn sapling and an oilskin on the ground beside it.

"You're not camping here, are you?" I asked.

"Not exactly."

"What *is* happening? Oh, Simon, it's been awful, —" and without warning I began to cry, snuffling into the back of my hand like a child because nowhere did I seem to have a handkerchief.

He put his arms round me and rocked me to and fro for a while until I calmed down and remembered that I had to tell him about Max. It appeared that Simon already knew he was looking for him.

"He mustn't find me, Sarah. He tried to kill me once."

"I know. I'm going to the police."

"You're *not!*" He pulled me down on to the oilskin and we sat close together, Simon enclosing my wrist in a tight grip as if to prevent me rushing off there and then. "The police know everything. I agreed to keep quiet and out of sight until they found out everything about everyone connected with this racket. It was important that Max should think his murder attempt had succeeded."

"And you wrote to tell us?"

"Yes. Well, not everything — I just said that you weren't to worry if you didn't hear from me for a while. It was the worst possible luck that the letter didn't get to you. You must have felt —" He broke off and sat staring at me for a moment. A savage look came into his eyes. "Jessica!" he said. "It was her fault! She didn't post the letter! God, I'll kill her!"

I gazed at him with my mouth open, totally bewildered.

"What's Jessica got to do with it?"

"Everything," he said grimly. "She's ruled me with a rod of iron these past six months."

"Simon," I begged, "will you please explain? What happened in Cannes and why are you here? And why do you have to hide like this and what in heaven's name has it all got to do with Jessica?"

"I'd better just start at the beginning," Simon said. "You know all about how I met Paul and Ted at the Sailing Club. What I didn't realise was that they and Max were in a drug-smuggling syndicate. They were to pick up a big consignment at Marseilles. I wasn't supposed to know, but Paul let it out one night and we had an almighty argument. I didn't want any part of it, as you can imagine, so I said they could let me off at Marseilles and I would make my own way home. It was sheer chance that I met the other two guys in a café — I'd intended to hitch-hike back by road until that point." He looked bleak for a moment. "That was their misfortune, poor devils."

"What happened in Cannes?"

"We'd tied up to take on provisions and get a new gas cylinder. Mike — that's one of the other guys — had just taken it aboard when he said he'd forgotten to pick up some anti-histamine stuff from the pharmacy. Johnny was a great big tough guy but he suffered from various allergies and was desperate for the stuff, so I said I'd go back for it, and off I went. I was on the way back when I saw Ted kind of lurking by a wall on the quayside. Funny, I thought. They were supposed to be heading back to England after Marseilles.

126

"I stopped and watched him for a moment, wondering where they were tied up, and then I saw Max sauntering along the quay with his hands in his pockets. He and Ted couldn't have avoided seeing each other, but they made no sign of recognition. It made me very suspicious. I figured that the sooner we left Cannes the better and I started back to the *Carissima* — that was the name of our boat — when suddenly there was the most awful bang and explosion and bits of things flying about in every direction, and that was the end of the *Carissima*. People were tearing down towards her and there were a couple of gendarmes racing down the quay blowing whistles. It was all total confusion. I just leaned against a wall trembling like a leaf and feeling horribly sick, thinking what must have happened to Mike and Johnny and knowing that my life wouldn't be worth a damn if Max found out that I hadn't gone up with them."

"Was he still hanging around?"

"I couldn't see either of them any more. Somehow they must have substituted a faulty cylinder — tampered with it in some way, I suppose — and got out fast the moment they saw it explode. I imagined that they'd get out of France and back to England right away, and that the best thing I could do was to go back too, rather than attempt any explanations in my atrocious French. It seemed to me that the British police would be the right ones to tell."

"So you managed to get a lift to Cornwall?"

"Right. I'd heard someone talking in the pharmacy only minutes before about leaving on the tide that afternoon, so I rushed back and managed to find them and they agreed to take me to Falmouth. I reported everything to the police the moment I arrived. I think they thought I was slightly mad, but I was passed from hand to hand and finally ended up with this steely-eyed, grey-haired copper with a mouth like a rat-trap who said they had reason to believe that this was part of a wider ring and that the CID were co-operating with the French police and would I co-operate too by kindly staying dead, thereby lulling Max and Co. into a false sense of security."

"Where does Jessica come into it?"

"Well, her husband had been a copper too, and he and this grim-faced character I mentioned had evidently been mates way-back-when, long before the Trewarthas went to Hong Kong and reached all sorts of dizzy heights. This guy — his name's Warburton — still keeps in touch with Jessica, and when there was a question of what to do with me he thought of her. He knew she had this big mansion, you see, and various other odd properties —"

"So you *were* in the Folly!"

"On and off, depending on where she had workmen at the time. Most of the winter I spent in the west wing, but the builders moved in there in a big way a month or so ago, so I moved out."

"And you gave her a letter to post? How could she not have sent it! What an unforgivable thing to do!"

The more I thought about her action, the angrier I became, but Simon had simmered down a little.

"I know she thought it unwise. Jessica is the complete policeman's wife, you know — duty above all things is the watchword. She'd been told to keep my presence a secret and she obeyed to the letter."

"Even so, she had no right to prevent you telling your family. How did she think we were feeling?"

"I'm so sorry, Sal."

Simon caught hold of my waist again, but gently

this time, and gave it a squeeze.

"I'm very angry with her," I said.

"So am I — in a way. On the other hand, I have no doubt she acted from the most laudable motives. And she did look after me very well."

"Laudable motives, eh?" Suddenly I had remembered what Jessica had said to me earlier concerning men and age and love being the very devil. "My guess is that she wanted to keep you to herself. She fancies you, doesn't she?"

He blushed scarlet, a sight so unusual that I looked at him in amazement.

"Good Lord," I murmured. "I think I hit the nail on the head."

"I can't help it," he said gruffly. "We've been thrown together an awful lot."

"You don't mean that *you* —?"

"Heavens above, what do you take me for? She's old enough to be my mother! She must have been a knock-out in her day, of course, but that day's long over, you have to admit."

"Poor Jessica," I said, changing my tune. I meant it, too. I had a sudden, sad knowledge of how she would feel once Simon had gone, once she had faced the certainty that it simply wasn't possible for her to excite the interest of a young man any more.

"Tell me, what were you doing scampering about down in Lamladroc Bay?" Simon asked, dismissing the subject of Jessica as of minor importance. "Didn't you see the 'Danger' notice?"

"No. I was too busy looking at the boat. Did you know it belongs to your friend Paul? I went down to see if I could sabotage his dinghy."

Simon laughed.

"I always knew you were ruthless. The dinghy happens to be inflatable and he took it away with him."

"He couldn't have," I said, after a moment's thought. "An old boy who spoke to me on the cliff said that you could only get into Lamladroc at high tide — and at high tide there was no way Paul could climb up the cliff carrying an inflatable dinghy."

"Your old boy didn't tell you that a really skilful sailor can make it through a narrow channel up to three hours before high tide?"

"He seemed to think that whoever moored that cutter there didn't have a clue."

"Then he was wrong. I saw Paul come in and it was as neat a piece of navigation as I ever saw. He's a total nit, is Paul, but he knows his boats."

"He doesn't seem the sort."

"Evidently he was in the Navy but was in trouble with the police and politely asked to leave. So he got himself taken on at the Sailing Club doing general maintenance after he came out of prison and worked his way up from there. I gather he's always been mad about boats. I'm not surprised that he's spent his ill-gotten gains on that beauty out there."

"How do you know so much about this coast?"

"Jessica's house is full of old books and charts. On every chart, Lamladroc was marked as unnavigable except at high tide, but on one dated 1786 someone had marked the channel in ink, all brown with age now, of course, and there was a note in the margin — something to the effect that the passage should be 'learned well and its secret consigned to the grave' as if whoever had marked it didn't want to share his knowledge with anyone. But obviously it wasn't consigned to any grave. Not that it matters now, for its clearly marked on all up-to-date charts, but from what your old boy said it sounds as if the myth survives and that local boatmen avoid the place."

"How fascinating! Why would anyone want to keep it secret. Would he have been smuggling too?"

"Very likely — but with a cargo less harmful than the heroin Max's boys were bringing in. Tell me, how's Lynn? Has her divorce come through?"

"Yes — she's a free woman and much happier. Simon, why did you go into the village last Sunday?"

"Because I was bloody starving! Jessica went away for a few days. I was holed up in the Folly and couldn't move because the place was swarming with workmen. Apart from not posting letters, Jessica has one other grievous fault. She eats like a bird herself and expects others to do likewise. Her idea of a square meal is a slice of crispbread lightly brushed with cottage cheese.

"Anyway, there I was, hungry as a hunter, with no chance of getting any more food until Jessica came back, so I thought I'd risk a quick dash to the village. There didn't seem much harm in it. I didn't think there would be many people about on a Sunday morning, but of course I reckoned without that moronic child and his parents and the TV crew. That really stirred up a hornets' nest! You and Max, not to mention Jessica and her copper friend having hysterics all over the place. It would have been far less bother to everyone if I'd stayed quietly in the Folly and starved to death."

"Where are you sleeping tonight?"

"Supposedly at the Manor, but I wish I didn't have to. I have a suspicion Max is on to it. Jessica said that someone was prowling around yesterday —"

"With binoculars. Someone was at the Folly, looking down at the beach."

"It wasn't me and it wasn't Jessica."

"She said it could have been a birdwatcher."

"I know. But she doesn't really believe it."

131

"Simon, don't go back there," I said. "Come to the Mill Cottage. I know Ben won't mind —"

"Benedict Farrell? Do you know him? Jessica told me he was living there."

"I've got to know him quite well over the last day or two. He's been wonderfully helpful — a terrific support to me."

The tone in which I spoke these harmless words must have spoken volumes, for Simon gave me a quizzical look, which I ignored.

"What could be more appropriate than taking shelter at the Mill Cottage?" I asked.

"What indeed? Well, OK, if you're sure he won't mind. I'd prefer it to going back to the Manor, I must admit . . . what time should I present myself? I might be quite late. I'd planned on sticking around here for a bit to see if there's any more activity with the cutter."

"Do be careful!"

"I'm always careful. Well, nearly always. I know my way about these cliffs blindfold and never show myself on the open road in daylight. Look what happened when I did."

"I'll go and prepare Ben for the fact that he's going to have a house-guest," I said. "When you say you'll be late, how late did you mean?"

Simon shrugged.

"Nineish — tenish, it's hard to say. Actually, you weren't the only one with designs on that cutter down there. I thought of waiting until low tide, then going aboard to take the bung out."

"Take care," I said again.

"You can count on it. Hey, Sarah —" I was getting up to leave, but at this sat down again. "Reading old books wasn't the only thing I did this winter. I actually finished a novel — yes, *finished* it! Jessica

132

lent me a typewriter, bought me paper; it was marvellous, really, having practically nothing else to do and no distractions. It was just what I needed."

"Simon, that's wonderful!" I said.

"Well, I don't suppose so. Actually, I've got no way of knowing if the thing's got any merit at all, but at least I finished it, which is pretty damned marvellous in itself, when you think of the number of times I've got to Chapter Five and stopped dead." He grinned at me, pleased with himself at his achievement, yet diffident at the same time. "I wonder if your friend Benedict Farrell would cast his eye over it for me? He might at least be able to tell me if it's remotely saleable, or just a load of rubbish."

"I'll ask him," I said. "But now I think I ought to go, Simon. I don't like this mist that's rolling in. I wish you would come with me."

Patches of sea mist like puffs of smoke were beginning to reach us, eerie and silent and dankly oppressive.

"Yes," Simon agreed. "You ought to go. It's amazing how quickly it comes in on an evening like this. But don't worry about me – as I said, I know this place blindfold by this time."

I disliked the idea of leaving him but was cheered by the thought that he would turn up at the Mill Cottage later. I drove straight there to tell Ben about it, only to find that the place was empty and he had not yet arrived home from Plymouth.

I was disappointed, but when I returned to my room at the Anchor and saw my dishevelled appearance reflected in the mirror I was rather glad that I had an opportunity to have a hot bath and wash my hair before seeing him. Always, at the back of my mind, was the thought of the beautiful women his name had been linked with in the past. I knew that I couldn't really compete, but at least there was no need to appear before him looking like a refugee from a hippy colony.

To this end I groomed myself and made up more carefully than usual, wishing as I did so that I had been a little less economical in my packing. I felt like celebrating having seen Simon at last and thought longingly of the clothes I had left in the cupboard at my flat. However, they were in Putney and I was in Poldrissick, so there was nothing for it but to put on clean jeans and the rather nice Italian batwing sweater that I had bought, with a slight rush of blood to the head, after my last pay-day.

That would have to do, I thought, as I surveyed myself before going once more to the cottage. And, all in all, it wasn't bad. Happiness had given me a glow that even I could see enhanced my looks and not even the thought that Ben had been disporting himself all day with the loveliest girls in the south-west could dampen my spirits. Simon was alive and well and nothing else — not even the thought of the danger that still threatened him — could quench my optimism that night.

This time Ben's car was outside the cottage, much to my relief. I knocked on the door. It was a black night, with mist swirling in the hollow which held the small house, and I hoped that Simon wouldn't wait too long on the cliff. I could think of nothing more dismal in weather like that.

I hardly noticed that Ben was less exuberant than usual. I was so full of everything that had happened that day that I babbled on without registering that he simply sat and looked at me in a most characteristic silence.

"You don't mind that Simon's coming here, do you?" I asked at last in a small voice when finally his lack of participation dawned on me.

"No, of course not. But you must have been crazy to go down to the beach without taking note of the tide. A child would appreciate the danger."

I looked at him, feeling deflated.

"I know," I said. "It just seemed like a good idea at the time. Simon was cross about it, too, but thank heaven he was there to get me up the cliff. Do you know, I forgot to tell him about Pierre Cloutier? I wish I'd thought of it."

"Who?"

"Pierre Cloutier. Oh, sorry, didn't I tell you about him? Well, Max had a phone call from him and I'm certain he must be connected with the drugs racket too because Paul implied that Max had to do what Cloutier told him. But then when I questioned him, he was awfully evasive —"

"Questioned who?" Ben pressed his hand against his forehead. "Look, I'm not really with it, Sarah. I'm pretty tired. It's been an awful, nightmarish sort of a day and the drive back was like something out of a horror movie, everywhere shrouded in mist, everyone still insisting on driving much too fast."

"I see," I said, and was silent, staring down at my hands. He's used up his quota of charm for today, I thought. He's been smiling and listening to people telling him how wonderful he is and asking him how he can bear to leave the stage, and now he's back here with an audience of one. After the role of superstar, he doesn't like it one bit. How right Jessica was, and how thankful I am that I haven't fallen in love with him — not in the slightest. Give me someone *ordinary*, I thought.

"How are you on omelettes?" he asked.

"Omelettes?" I looked up at him in astonishment. He was smiling apologetically. "Omelettes? Oh, pretty good."

"Then be an angel and whip one up for me, will you? I'll have an extra large Scotch to restore me and turn me into human being again, and then I'll be fit to talk to. Honestly, it's been a *pig* of a day. I don't know when I've been more exhausted. If ever anything was designed to make me realise that I've made the right decision, then today was it."

"Really?"

"Really!" He got up from his chair to pour himself the promised drink. "And I'm starving, so get beating, girl."

"Didn't they feed you at this shindig of yours?"

"There was an enormous spread laid out, but I left early. I found, somewhat to my surprise, that I wanted to get back to you."

"Oh." I stood and looked at him, knowing that I was grinning like an idiot, but not caring. He was glad to be back! He wasn't bored, he hadn't lost interest. He was merely tired after a hard day and an exhausting journey, and what could be more ordinary than that?

I was singing to myself as I tied a blue-and-white striped apron round my waist.

"Can you find everything?" he called from the living-room.

"I think so." There was cheese and the makings of a salad. The bread was stale but would be all right toasted.

"I'll just go and get some logs for the fire," he said. I heard him go outside and come back again. I heard him talking to the dog. His voice sounded lazy and contented. He put a record on – Beethoven, I think it was. Anyway, it was something grand and melodic and it made me feel good. One omelette was slightly less than perfect, but, naturally, I gave Ben the good one and he was loud in his praise.

And I was happy because no matter what the feminists say, there's something primevally satisfying about making a meal for the man one loves.

There, I said to myself. You've admitted it.

We were sitting by the fire, eating from trays on our laps, and I concentrated hard on the meal in front of me, not letting my glance stray towards Ben as I felt sure that this revelation would be clear for him to see. We sat in silence with the music washing over us. At last he put the tray down on the table at his side and gave a long, satisfied sigh.

"Better?"

"Much. Thanks, Sarah."

"I needed it, too."

"I didn't only mean the food. There's something so calming and peaceful about being with you. A girl who knows when to be quiet is a delightful rarity in my experience. The trouble with the acting profession in general is that the members of it seldom know when to stop giving a performance."

"Sit there," I said, getting up and taking his tray. "I'll take my delightful silence into the kitchen to make coffee."

"Wonderful!" He leaned forward and gripped my wrist as I bent over the table at his side, preventing me from moving. "I couldn't be happier about Simon, Sarah. I'm sorry I was such a wet blanket."

"You were tired," I said, very conscious of his touch.

"Even so, I'm sorry. I've always reserved a very special sort of dislike for wet blankets. I can't bear people who don't rejoice when their friends rejoice."

"And weep when they weep?"

He smiled at me and lifted my wrist to his lips.

"I'm glad I haven't got to weep for you."

So what about Jessica's warning now, I asked

137

myself, as I stood waiting for the coffee to percolate. Five minutes ago she was absolutely right, her advice sound. Now you're ready to throw it out of the window. Oh, but he's so *nice*, my heart cried. So nice, so warm, so *involved* in all one's hopes and fears.

His voice came to me from the open doorway, bringing me back to reality with a jump.

"Do you want to phone your sister?"

It was typical of him to suggest it. I longed to pass on the good news, but I hesitated to do so.

"Let's wait until Simon's here," I said. "Then he can tell her himself."

We drank our coffee, sitting by the fire not in silence this time but with conversation easy between us. He told me about his day. Yes, of course, everyone had been asking him if he'd ever go back to acting, whether he didn't miss the excitement. Everybody always did. He was sick to death of explaining himself! Why did people care so much?

Because he'd commanded their love, I told him. He'd entertained them, made them laugh, reduced them to tears. He'd become part of their life.

It was so good to have time to talk, time to explore each other's hearts and minds. He got up and one point to let the dog out and stood by the open door, breathing the night air as if he couldn't get enough of it.

"Come here," he said, holding out an arm towards me. I joined him at the door, and he held me close to him. "The mist seems to have lifted. Just smell the damp earth and the woodsmoke and the faint aroma of cows. I feel as if I never want to leave this place again."

"And to think," I said, "that I drenched myself in Chanel entirely for your benefit!"

138

He laughed and pulled me even closer.

"Now that you mention it, I perceive that it's very pleasant." He buried his face in the curve of my neck. "Mm. Not to say titillating. Anyway, it's sure as hell preferable to diesel fumes. You can keep your nasty, dirty, smelly towns with all their nasty, dirty, noisy traffic."

"And you really won't miss the smell of the greasepaint and the roar of the crowd?"

"You can keep that, too. This afternoon gave me a small reminder of what my past life was like. It was fine for about the first half-hour, but after that I couldn't wait to come back to the cottage and my desk and the peace and quiet of the country-side. Knowing that I'd be seeing you didn't hurt one bit, either. Come on — let's shut the night out and get back to the fire."

But I stayed for a moment staring out into the darkness. Where was Simon? Surely it was time for him to be here. But he had said he might be late, so it would be foolish to worry about him. Besides, Ben was waiting for me inside that cosy room.

By mutual consent we neither of us went back to our own chairs, but sat together on the leather chesterfield, Ben's arm around my shoulders. He asked me to tell him all over again about my talk with Max and my meeting with Paul, and I did so. It was when I was once more embarking on a des-cription of my emotions on seeing the unknown pair of denim jeans coming down the cliff towards me that I perceived that he was no longer listening, even though his eyes were on me. I stopped in mid-sentence.

"Has anyone ever told you that you have a sin-gularly enchanting dimple in your cheek that comes and goes when you talk?" he asked.

"It has been said."

"And your eyelashes have gold flecks at the end of them." .

I looked at him, wondering if his heart was pounding like mine, feeling sure that it couldn't possibly be, for if it had been he could never have found the breath to frame such pretty speeches. But then he bent to kiss me, holding me closely, and then I knew that his heart was pounding every bit as quickly as my own.

"You're so sweet," he said huskily at last.

"With such a nice little face!" I was laughing at him.

"It's a *lovely* face. It's the sort that grows on you, the sort that you don't get tired of."

"How can you possibly know that?"

"Instinct. Experience. Native wisdom." He punctuated these expressions with three brief kisses.

Could it really be possible? It felt so good, just being with him, just knowing he was there to depend on. I leaned against him for a moment, saying nothing, merely luxuriating mindlessly in the happy present, not probing into what the future might hold.

He kissed me again, a long, lingering kiss that left us both shaken, not smiling now, both wanting more.

"If it weren't for the fact that your brother might be here at any moment —"

I sat up.

"Ben — Simon should surely be here by now! What's the time, for heaven's sake? He said he'd be late, but I can't imagine he'd be as late as this."

Reluctantly Ben looked at his watch, startled when he saw the time.

"It's almost half past ten," he said. "I'd no idea —"

"It's true he wasn't very specific about the exact time he'd come, but I'm sure he meant to be here before this. Ben, I'm worried. Something could have happened to him. He said that Max had been snooping around the Manor. Suppose he found Simon after all?"

He ran his fingers through his hair as if at the same time trying to create order in his added wits.

"Maybe we should give him a little longer before we panic —"

"But it's hours since I saw him! Anything could have happened. Maybe Max has got him and intends taking him out on the cutter tonight."

"Wait. Let's think. It was high tide around four o'clock, wasn't it?"

I nodded, sure of my facts. How could I ever forget the sight of those waves rolling in and covering the rocks that were my only way out of Lamladroc?

"Then it will be low tide now. Perhaps just on the turn. Even if Max has got Simon, there's no way he can leave the cove before, say, twelve-thirty."

"Two hours!"

"There's another possibility, Sarah. Simon could have fallen. The mist was thick, remember. I know he said that he could find his way blindfold, but anyone could slip and break an ankle."

My hand flew to my mouth.

"Those awful cliffs!"

"He'd have enough sense to keep away from them, surely. I was thinking of the ditches and gates and all the obstacles he'd have to overcome between Lamladroc and here, especially if he comes over the fields and keeps away from the roads. Perhaps we should give him a little longer."

"We *must* tell the police."

"Simon wouldn't thank us for panicking before it was strictly necessary. What might be a good idea, perhaps, is to ring Jessica. She might have a number to ring in an emergency. Not that I'm ready to concede that this *is* an emergency just yet, so try to keep calm."

I went 'to the door again and looked out into the dark night. It was all very still and silent.

Ben came up behind me and put his hand on my shoulder.

"I'll go up the meadow towards the track and the Home Farm, just to have a scout around. As I said, he might have fallen."

"I'll come too —"

"No. You stay here. And if I'm not back in twenty minutes, phone Jessica and tell her you're worried. Maybe she's worried, too. After all, he was supposed to go back to the Manor tonight so unless he got a message to her, she'll be wondering what's up."

I hated to see him go. I stood and watched as the darkness swallowed him up, then reluctantly closed the door and returned once more to the room where, unthinkingly, I had been happy only a few minutes before.

TEN

By eleven o'clock he had not returned and I was about to phone Jessica when I heard the dog barking and the sound of footsteps on the flagstones outside. Hopefully, I rushed outside but Ben was alone.

"Still not here?" he asked me. "I saw no sign of him, either."

He went straight to the phone and dialled Jessica's number, chewing his lip impatiently as he waited for her to answer the call. He waited and waited, then put down the receiver.

"No reply," he said. "She must be out to dinner, or something."

"So now what do we do?"

"I'll ring the police. What was the name of the man who's in charge of all of this operation? Did Simon mention it?"

"Yes, he did." I screwed up my face in an effort to remember. I beat my fist against my forehead. "Damn it all, what on earth was it? It was something quite long. Something beginning with a W — "

It was hopeless. Wilberforce? Warrington? Westonbirt? No, that was the name of the colonel who lived in the lodge.

"I just can't remember," I said miserably.

"Never mind. Perhaps it won't matter."

Ben spoke to a slow-speaking and rather bored sounding constable at Falmouth Police Station, who appeared to regard his potted version of events with a tolerant incredulity.

"It's a missing person you want to report, is it,

sir?" I could hear the voice clearly as I huddled close to the phone.

"More than that. We've reason to believe that the man is in danger."

"Oh, yes, sir? What sort of danger would that be?"

"Look, this is rather a time-wasting exercise, Constable. Can you give me the number of the man in charge of investigations into drug-smuggling?"

There was a short silence from the other end of the telephone.

"Perhaps you'd be wanting Customs and Excise, sir."

Exasperatedly Ben turned his eyes to heaven.

"I want some help from the police," he said, managing with an effort to keep his voice calm. "Can you please put me on to your superior — "

"It is rather late, sir. Unless this is an emergency, it would be best to file a report and contact the Station Superintendant in the morning."

"This *is* an emergency! I've told you, a man is in danger. His name is Simon Kendall and your people apparently know all about him."

"Hang on a moment, sir. I'll see if we have any record — "

Ben hung on, silently pounding the desk with his fist, his impatience growing by the second. The constable returned.

"I'm sorry, sir. We don't seem to have any record of a Mr Simon Kendall."

"Because he was in hiding." Ben was speaking very precisely, every word clearly articulated. "He was in hiding at the instigation of your drug squad."

"Tell you what, sir. Leave your name and number and I'll get back to you. It's more than my job's worth to disturb the Super over every crank that calls — beg your pardon, sir, but I'm sure you understand."

Ben was looking at his watch as the man spoke.

"Don't bother ringing back," he said succinctly. "Just tell your Super that if anyone's interested in seeing Simon Kendall alive again, they ought to be at Lamladroc Cove any time during the next hour."

He dropped the receiver back on to its rest.

"We can't waste any more time with that," he said. "We must get there ourselves. Let's hope the message gets through."

"If only I could remember the name!"

"If only Jessica wasn't out. If only I hadn't wasted time going to look for him."

"Maybe Jessica's back by now."

He phoned her again, with the same result. She had not returned.

He wasted no more time. We both reached for our coats and made for Ben's car and very soon were jouncing up the track towards the road.

We saw no one, neither on the road nor at the point where the footpath to Lamladroc joined it. There were still little pockets of swirling mist in the dips and hollows, but the sky above us was thick with stars.

Ben drove the car slowly past the footpath until we reached a field with a five-barred gate. I got out to open it and he drove inside, leaving the car hidden behind a hedge. All was still and silent. Uneasily I looked around. There were deep shadows close to the hedge, strange shapes made even stranger by the mist which wreathed about them.

Ben took my hand and together we walked back along the lane until we reached the footpath. It seemed as if we were the last people left alive on the earth; as if the mist had created a world of fantasy which could well be inhabited, not by humans,

145

but by weird creatures never seen outside childhood tales of demons and sorcerers.

If that were true here, it was more than ever so
when we reached the part where the gorse grew
high above us. It was pitch-dark here, dark and
misty. Silence seemed to press in on us from both
sides. Ben produced a small torch from his pocket,
which he used with caution, but because of the
strangely shifting movement of the mist it enhanced
the feeling of other worldliness rather than dispelled it.

There were rustlings from the vegetation at the
side of the path, the sudden flick of a rabbit's scut
on the path ahead, eyes which gleamed in the light
of the torch and disappeared.

We came out of the darkness on to the bare cliff,
which, in contrast, seemed almost as light as day.
We could see the white edge on the waves and the
lights of Poldrissick gleaming away to the south-
west.

Cautiously Ben held me back and looked to
right and left before stepping out of the shadow
of the bushes. Still we seemed to have the world
to ourselves. Only the heaving, murmuring sea beneath us sang its continuous, background song.

We continued along the path, which shone whitely
like a livid scar in the sloping hillside, following
the contours of the cliff. In Indian file we followed
it, feeling horribly exposed. It was a relief to plunge
into the shadow of the bushes once more, even
though the wreathing mist was heavy here and we
had to slow the pace of our footsteps.

"Ben, I hope we're right," I breathed softly.
"Simon said he would try to sink the boat. Suppose
he did! Suppose they've taken him somewhere else!"

"It's there."

We had emerged on to the cliff at the point where

I had earlier seen the old man. The cutter was still riding at anchor. I hardly knew whether to be glad or sorry, for it surely meant that Max and Paul must have taken Simon before he had been able to harm it. On the credit side, it implied that they would still choose this way of disposing of him. At least we were here, and in time.

Ben leaned close.

"There's still at least half an hour before they could sail out of the cove," he said. "And about three hours after that before it's high tide. We still have some time to play with."

"They're not here yet."

"We don't know that." He was silent for a moment, looking and listening. "I admit there's no sign of them. I think we should get down there. There's only the one way down, over the rocks. If we're there in advance, waiting for them, we can hide ourselves in the shadows at the bottom. Maybe I should have provided myself with some sort of weapon."

"There are plenty of rocks."

"That's true. I think I prefer to rely on my rugger tackle, though. Our biggest weapon will be surprise."

I swallowed with difficulty. There was something remarkably unappealing about stepping out of the shadow of the bushes on to the grassy cliff where anyone watching could clearly see us against the skyline. It never occurred to me not to go with him, though, and I was grateful that it didn't seem to occur to him either.

"Come on," he said.

He led me round to the easy descent and without speaking he helped me down, first the steeper section, and then the more gentle passage across the rocks. From time to time we stopped and scanned the cliffs.

There was no sign of anyone. No movement, except the surging and retreating sea.

He jumped down to the beach and turned to hold out a hand to me.

"Just hold it right there!"

The menacing voice growled at us out of the darkness. I gasped and clung to the rock, still two or three feet above the level of the beach. Startled, Ben turned his head and suddenly we saw figures detaching themselves from the shadows all round the bay converging upon us.

The man who had spoken was tall and broad, and he had a rifle jammed between Ben's shoulder-blades. I tried to shout but was unable to utter a word. Rough hands pulled me down and a light was shone into my face so that I blinked and twisted my head away from it.

"Just see 'oo 'tis," someone said softly. "'Tis the maid 'oo likes to ask questions."

With my eyes blinded by the light I tried to peer into the darkness. There was something familiar about the voice.

Ben, pale with shock, was standing with his hands up, but at this he gave a soft laugh and lowered them.

"Jack Watkin," he said, turning round and pushing the rifle to one side. "Just what the hell do you think you're about? What's the idea of frightening us to death?"

"We thought maybe 'twas a pair of kids from St Petra," Jack Watkin said, his voice sulky. "Come 'ere for a bit 'o you-know-what. We only wanted to scare 'em off, like. They people over to St. Petra, too bloomin' nosy about our business, they are."

"And what is your business, Jack?" Ben asked softly. "It wouldn't be smuggling, would it?"

Another figure loomed up and I recognised with

148

a feeling of inevitability that it was Laurie Barron.

"Don't answer that," he said. "I don't know what Miss Kendall's game is, but she and her brother are too bloody nosy for my liking, never mind the St Petra folk."

"Douse that light," someone growled from the shadows. "The Frenchie's out there. 'E'll think it safe to come in."

All eyes turned to look out to sea. Away in the darkness there was a pinprick of light which disappeared as suddenly as it had come. In silence everyone watched, and again the light pierced the darkness only to disappear again.

"'Tis the Frenchie right enough," Jack Watkin said.

"Bringing what?" Ben asked.

"Tidn't none of your business. Better fit you 'adn't seen nothing."

" 'Watch the wall, my darling, as the gentlemen go by,' " Ben quoted.

"Eh?"

"Just a line of poetry, Jack. It's an old game, isn't it?"

I thought of the chart Simon had mentioned — the chart giving the passage with the instructions that it should be kept a secret. An old game, indeed — but was it still 'Brandy for the parson, baccy for the clerk' that came this way? A cold hand seemed to clutch at my heart. Were Jack and Laurie and all the others somehow involved with Max, too? If so, we were doomed, and so was Simon.

Laurie came over and looked down at me, powerful and menacing.

"I suppose," he said, "you're going to tell me that you're down here looking for your brother?" His voice had a jeering ring to it and I could see his smile gleaming at me in the darkness.

"She is, Laurie," Ben said, before I could speak. "And so am I. Any minute now some very unpleasant characters are going to bring him down here and take him out to that cutter for a little sail. It's our guess they don't intend to bring him back again."

There was a moment's silence.

"Pull the other one," Laurie said.

"It's true. Jack, for God's sake stop waving that rifle about!"

"'Tis only an old airgun, Mr. Farrell. 'Twouldn't do nobody any 'arm — just window-dressing, as you might say."

"Just keep it down. And there's something else you ought to know. We left a message for the police to come down here to rescue him, so they could be here any time."

Laurie swore softly.

"The Frenchie can't come in for another thirty minutes. He's standing off till we show a light."

"What *do* you bring in, Laurie?"

"Nothing much."

"Drugs?"

"Never!"

"Don't trust him, Ben," I said urgently. "He could be in it with Max."

Ben laughed.

"Somehow I don't think so. Poldrissick men don't even co-operate with their neighbours in St. Petra, still less with 'furriners' like Max. Isn't that so, Laurie?"

"I never heard of anyone called Max."

"He's bad. He's got to be stopped."

Laurie stood, his legs astride, looking long and silently out to sea where now no light shone. The other shadowy figures grouped themselves around

150

him. Even there in the darkness there was no mistaking that he was the leader of this little band.

"You could help, Laurie. He's not so choosy as you. He smuggles drugs and Sarah's brother is likely to die because he knows too much. It's as simple as that." Ben's voice was low and persuasive.

Still Laurie gazed out to sea and said nothing. There were sighs and mutterings among the others.

"All they beauties out there," Jack Watkin murmured regretfully.

"Beauties?" For one moment I had a bizarre picture of a kind of floating harem, filled with glamorous French girls.

"Ar. Some beautiful they are."

"What's he talking about, Laurie?" Ben asked again, his voice tinged with amusement.

I saw Laurie shrug. He gave a short laugh.

"Oysters," he said. "You might as well know, seeing there won't be any more coming in after tonight's little fiasco."

"*Oysters*? Why in the name of everything holy should anyone smuggle oysters into Cornwall? We've got a pretty good export industry here — "

"That's it, mate. We take them in so that they can be shipped out again."

"I don't get it."

Laurie sighed.

"Neither will we, after tonight. There's this chap, see, over in Brittany with thousands of francs tied up in oyster-beds. Remember that big oil spillage last spring? The French government slapped an order on him stopping any sale for two years, because they said they could be contaminated. Absolute codswallop, that is. Nothing but blasted beaurocracy and red tape. The oil never reached him in any quantity, but there's no way they'll lift the order,

151

even though he's eaten a dozen of his own oysters sitting on the pavement outside the Ministry of Ag. and Fish, or whatever it's called over there. He reckons it's all political. Someone wants him out of business so that they can build hotels all along his strip of the estuary."

I listened, bemused, only half taking in this story. It all sounded highly unlikely to me. Oysters? It was almost laughable, set against the murky, lethal business carried on by Max and his friends. Ben, as always, was intrigued.

"So he sends his oysters to you, and you resell them as Helford oysters?"

"Something like that."

"*What* a nice little racket!"

"Ben," I said, tugging his sleeve. "They'll be here soon for certain."

He abandoned all thought of the oysters and returned even more urgently to the problem that faced us.

"Are you going to help us, Laurie?"

"I think we ought to," Jack Watkin said, before Laurie could speak. "After all, Mr Farrell is one 'o we, say what you will, Laurie."

Laurie pushed his seaman's cap to the back of his head in a gesture of resignation.

"Doesn't look as if I've got much choice," he said. "You weren't having me on when you said that the police were coming?"

"I said they might be. We left word."

Laurie uttered a loud and lugubrious sigh.

"It breaks my heart to do it, but you'd better show the red light, Jack. We don't want the Frenchie putting in and finding the place swarming with fuzz, do we?"

Jack relayed the order to someone in the rear of

152

the group, who disappeared towards the rear of the beach, presumably to fetch a light.

"How do you get the oysters home?" Ben asked Laurie curiously.

"I sailed my tosher in here hours ago, well before low tide. We load her up and putt-putt back to harbour, no trouble to anyone, not like if the Frenchie came into Poldrissick. Cap'n Pengelly would have to sit up and take notice then." He raised his voice a little. "That's right, Bill. Two flashes, count of ten, two more. That'll send him on his way, more's the pity."

"I'm surprised it's worth it," Ben said.

Laurie laughed softly.

"There's a lot of money in oysters," he said. "Specially at give-away prices. The Frenchie's in no position to drive a hard bargain. Besides, we all enjoy the sport, don't we, boys?"

"Mrs Watkin doesn't enjoy it, does she?" I remembered suddenly the argument in the kitchen.

"A man's got to have his bit of excitement. I suppose you could say we've got smuggling in our blood. You're not going to shop us, are you?"

"Are you going to help us?" Ben asked.

Before Laurie could answer there was the sound of a shower of stones rattling down the cliff.

"They're here," Ben breathed. "How about it, Laurie? Your help in return for our silence?"

"Get the girl out of the way," Laurie said softly.

It was like some strange, macabre ballet, the way the shapes once more melted into the shadows. Ben gave me a small push towards the base of the cliff. Silent and alone I eased myself over and sank down on a small rock in the shelter of the overhang.

My eyes were accustomed to the darkness and I could see that Laurie, Jack and Ben were all pressed

153

against the rock, Jack and Ben to the right, Laurie to the left, above which anyone coming down to the beach had to pass. More stones rattled down but still there was no one in sight. The seconds ticked by. And then I could see them silhouetted against the night sky.

Paul was staggering unsteadily under the burden of the dinghy, which appeared to be strapped to his back. Simon, too, looked unsteady, which was hardly surprising as his arms were bound behind him and he was being urged along at gunpoint by Max. He looked like an awkward, wingless bird, unable to balance. At one stage he almost fell, but Max reached out and grabbed him, growling something inaudible.

The men on the beach waited patiently without a sound. The noise of the waves was increasing. I looked towards the sea, noting with a brief clutch of fear that the creamy foam was creeping up the beach at alarming speed. But the men knew what they were doing, I calmed myself. There must be plenty of time yet before our line of retreat was cut off.

And now at last the halting progress of the three on the rocks had brought them to within feet of that last leap on to the beach and I could see tensions in the line of the men's bodies underneath as they waited for the jump that would deliver Max and Paul into their hands.

It came, and suddenly the noise was deafening, the whole rock illuminated brilliantly as Laurie's helpers turned powerful flashlights on it, shouting and yelling in a way that brought my heart leaping into my mouth.

What it did for the other three I could only imagine. Paul's face was bone white as he pressed himself back against the rock, and Max stood as if turned to stone, the gun hanging limply in his hand, before Laurie brought him crashing to the ground in a grip that would have done credit to the Cornish wrestlers of old.

Only Simon looked happy. I stood up and yelled at him, and with Max and Paul both overpowered he would have come over to me had not Ben stopped him, producing a knife to cut the rope that tied his wrists. I went over and joined them, throwing my arms around Simon.

"Thank God," I said. "Thank God. I tried to keep believing that it would all end happily, but there were times when I doubted – "

"Then start doubting again," Simon said. "Here comes Warburton."

"*Warburton*! That was the name I couldn't think of."

"Lucky you," Simon murmured. "I think of little else."

There were lights and people in plenty now on the rocks above. The police were moving in, it seemed, and a grey-haired, slight man in a sheepskin coat came over and joined us.

"Well, Simon?" he said acidly.

"Look at it this way, Mr Warburton," Simon said. "It could be worse. I could be dead."

"There are times when I feel that might be a very happy solution. You realize what you've done, don't you? You've blown six months of patient work, that's all – not only on this side of the Channel, but in France, too. We nearly had them, boy. We so nearly had them."

"I'm sorry," Simon said humbly.

"Sorry?" I couldn't take any more of this. I turned to the wretched Warburton and gave him a withering look. "He's alive, Mr Warburton. And, as his sister, I find that very cheering."

"Shut up, Sal," Simon said wearily. "He's right. I blew the whole thing, just by going into the village that day. Just one mistake was enough."

"You've got Max," I said. Max and Paul were being handcuffed and marched away even as I spoke.

"We've known about him for a long time. We've been watching him. It's the French contact that remains elusive."

"What about Pierre Cloutier?" I asked.

Warburton turned towards me.

"Who?"

"Pierre Cloutier. He lives in Paris. I knew him as a business associate of Max's — I thought he was to do with the motor industry, but he phoned Max at his hotel in St Petra. Why would he have done that? He must have been just as worried as Max when he heard that Simon wasn't dead after all. That's my guess, anyway. And Max made it quite clear from his manner that Cloutier was the boss."

"Give me the name again," Warburton snapped.

I did so, and he repeated it softly.

"I think, Miss Kendall," he said, "that you may just have saved the day."

I could see Simon grinning at me in the darkness.

"Who's a clever girl, then?" he said.

I was the only one facing the sea, and once again I was suddenly conscious that it had inched considerably nearer to us.

"Er — the water's getting very close," I said nervously.

The three men turned, swore in unison, and four of us made a dash for the rocks.

"Just in time, or born in the vestry," Simon

yelled to me as we ran, and I laughed far more wildly than the joke deserved. It was so good to have him back.

ELEVEN

"I think it's very good," Ben said, handing Simon back the typescript of his novel."

"It needs an awful lot of revision, I know, and I'm not too happy about the way Carla comes over. I meant to make her a softer sort of character altogether."

"I enjoyed it. Honestly."

"I know it's pretty awful — I mean, not in your class, or anything. The first part is too long-drawn-out — " he stopped short as if he had only just registered Ben's words. "Did you really enjoy it?"

"I said so, didn't I?"

"You're not simply being kind?"

"Look, you asked me for an honest opinion, and I gave it. I enjoyed it very much."

Simon grinned from ear to ear.

"Well, that's great. That's wonderful! It makes six months in the wilderness really worth while. Did you hear that Sal? Benedict Farrell actually liked my book!" His smile died. "I don't suppose it's good enough to send to anyone, is it?"

"Certainly it is. Maybe you're right about the first part. It could do with pruning here and there, but having done that I'd be angry if you *didn't* send it to someone."

At this Simon stared down at the typescript in his hands, almost overcome. He cleared his throat.

"Thanks," he said gruffly. "Thanks an awful lot, Ben." He looked dazed, as if Ben's praise had taken his breath away. "I promised I'd tell Jessica what you thought. I must go and see if I can find her. She'll be as thrilled as I am." He muttered his thanks again and swiftly left us.

We were in the flat in the west wing of the Manor, where Simon and I had stayed together for the two nights that had passed since the happenings on the beach and the terrible night when Max and Paul had surprised Simon on the cliff, just as he was making his way to Mill Cottage. Mr Warburton had now declared us free to go home. We had spoken to Lynn on the phone and were all looking forward to a slap-up celebration of our reunion in the near future.

"I'm thrilled that you liked Simon's novel," I said to Ben. "You've made him so happy. It's nice that he wants to share it with Jessica."

"You've forgiven her for suppressing the letter?"

"I don't think I'll ever quite do that. It was a ruthless, monstrous, appalling thing to do — but I suppose she had Simon's welfare at heart as well as the police operation. He would have been in grave danger if word of his presence had leaked out, as events proved. He owes her quite a lot, really."

"It wasn't all one way." He came over to me. "Simon gave Jessica something, too. Obviously he didn't feel about her the way she felt about him, but he gave her a purpose in life at a time when she felt very much alone. It did her good to have someone to worry about and take care of and plan for, She'll miss him, of course, but in a way he's served his purpose. He made her come alive again."

"Well, that's a good thing." I spoke absently. I was thinking of what Jessica had said to me concerning Ben, and impulsively I told him. "She warned me against taking you seriously," I said.

He turned me to face him, putting his hands on my shoulders and bending to kiss me.

159

"I've never considered her the wisest of women."

I said nothing. I certainly had no wish to believe her, but could not rid myself of thoughts of all the beautiful women he had known in his glamorous past. Would they haunt me for ever, I wondered? I sighed.

"I can't help thinking that common sense is on her side, though," I said.

He laughed and drew away from me, studying me at arm's length.

"No one ever wrote sonnets to common sense," he said. "But I could quote you quite a few on the subject of love."

I laughed too, and shook my head.

"Oh, no, not that," I said. "It makes me tingle to hear you talking about cornflakes – Shakespeare would definitely be giving you an unfair advantage."

"I'll remember that." He pulled me close and I could feel his smiling lips moving softly over my hair. "I aim to make you tingle quite frequently."

It was my turn to study him. I looked up into his face and saw his strength and his kindness, his humour and intelligence, plus that extra, special, magic ingredient that seemed to endow him with a greater zest for life than anyone I had ever met. Suddenly forgetting him didn't seem like common sense after all.

I put my arms around his neck and reached up to kiss him.

"I'll be back, my handsome," I said. "My very, very, handsome."

He smiled at me and I seemed to see whole cohorts of imaginary beauties fade, wraith-like, in the bright and hopeful reality of our future together.